# THE TALEO CARTEL: THE INC.

## K. RENEE

# CHARACTER INSPIRATIONS

From the ruthless streets of Philadelphia comes the Taleo Cartel, a lucrative, formidable, and dangerous enterprise that is ran by two brothers with a tight fist.

After the head of the cartel passes down the reigns to his oldest twin son, Javari Taleo must step in and get all affairs in order. Aside from protecting his brother, who does the unthinkable, and then finding out his wife has been disloyal, Javari's back is forced up against the wall as the weight of the world rests on his shoulders. As fate would have it, a damsel in distress ends up being just what the doctor ordered, but is Javari able to put his trust in someone after all the disloyalty that's been revealed around him?

Jakari Taleo has always been known as the "smart, computer tech" twin. Being born just eight minutes after his older brother, Jakari enjoys living life under the radar. It's not until he finds himself in a compromising position that he finds out just what it's like walking in his brother's shoes. Together, Javari and Jakari must stick together as they attempt to infiltrate the justice system while still maintaining their territory.

In this jaw dropping story, be prepared for the inevitable as the Taleo Cartel takes over and proves their worthiness to not only the Inc. but to some of the most notorious cartels in the United States.

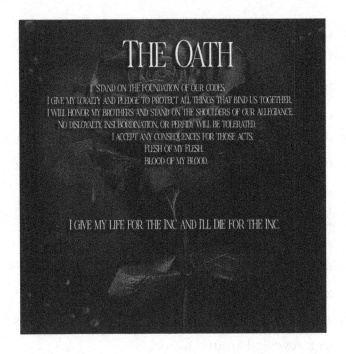

# JAVARI

---

**Loyalty - *Giving or showing firm and constant support or allegiance to a person or institution.***

---

LOYALTY IS *faithfulness to commitment or obligations.*

In my world, there is no fuckin' OR. You gon' be faithful to us, yo' ass gon' show commitment, and be obligated to whatever the fuck we're obligated to. Loyalty is a word that defines the deepest part of me. The meaning is heavy yet gentle enough to ease through the cracks of betrayal. In my line of work, it's a silent pact and an unspoken vow that's understood in the streets. It's a word I stand on, a word that will forever bind anyone who's a part of the Taleo Cartel. For us, loyalty isn't just a word; it's a determining factor of who lives or who dies. You either have it in you or you don't. I live by it, and if you break that bond with me, consider it your

1

death certificate. There isn't a place on this side of the globe that you can hide. I'll find you, and I'ma damn sure kill you.

Looking at my watch, it was a little after six in the morning, and instead of me doing my morning rituals of being knee-deep in my wife, answering some emails, and working out, I was sitting in the corner of this tiny ass bedroom watching this pussy ass nigga, and his bitch peacefully sleep. It's crazy how a nigga with all this money didn't have proper security in place to protect the dwelling that housed his family. An amateur for sure; this dude didn't learn shit from his pop. It took my brother Jakari only seconds to break through that ancient ass alarm system.

First thing any man in this game should always do, even if you're starting out as a corner boy, is to ensure that his family is protected and safe at all costs. From where I'm sitting right now, this nigga failed his family. For the last thirty minutes, I've been sitting in this corner, smoking on my Cuban, watching these niggas slob and snore without a care in the world. You would have thought that they would've smelled my cigar by now. Then this nigga had the nerve to be out here trying to put fear in the hearts of other muthafuckas, when he could be touched so easily. I'm sure if they knew how easy it was, somebody might've pulled his cap back a long time ago. The only reason they let him rock out is because of us.

Brock Zanardi, head of the Zanardi Cartel, came to my Pop right after his own dad was gunned down while he was in Cuba on business. Once he took the reins, many didn't think that he had what it took to keep the Zanardi Cartel intact. They'd lost so many business deals and close alliances because of it. He'd allowed others to move into their territory and ports without any repercussions. My Pop was devastated over his best friend's death, and rightfully so. So, when Jerimiah Zanardi's son came to him pleading for help, my Pop wasted no time stepping in and ensuring that he had the backing of the Taleo's. We indeed had his back, stood on the frontline for the Zanardi's. My pop put his name, time, and money on the line for the sake of his best friend's organization and the wellbeing of his family. Now we're here in this moment dealing with this disloyal piece of shit. Disrespecting me would always get you toe tagged, but disrespecting my Pop, after everything he's done for your ungrateful ass, that'll definitely get you an *expedited* toe tag. I didn't play when it came to my family.

Brock and his bitch decided loyalty wasn't something worth giving back. Not only did he betray us, but he had the nerve to team up with our biggest rival, the Sandoval Cartel, to plot and take us out. We planned to handle the Sandoval's soon, we just had some loose ends to tie up before we moved on that. Today was just his expiration date. In this game, I'd always tried to keep women and kids out of it, but every now and then, you had to make an example out of a bitch! Something to remind these muthafuckas who to play with and who not to play with. Because playing with the Taleo's is never the right decision. There are rules to this life.

Rule number one: Never bite the hand that keeps you the fuck breathing.

I'm the nigga that would cut your air supply off while you're out having dinner in the middle of a packed restaurant. The only reason I'm not on go the way I want to be is because my Pop runs the show. He's the boss of the Taleo's and disrespecting authority is something we'll never do. We show our ass every now and then just let these niggas know what it is. On some real shit, my way of running this organization would be different than the way my father runs it. We're in a new day and age, times have changed, and you have to show these muthafuckas in different ways not to ever fuck with you. Running a Cartel is like playing chess. Your moves have to be calculated, and you're thinking three steps ahead. This ain't no street operation shit. I'm not standing on a street corner in the middle of the hood, and I damn sure don't have street corner wars. This Cartel shit is more sophisticated than that. We move with ease and stand on business when it comes to our organization. But don't ever get it twisted; I'll step out of this Armani suit and these Tom Ford shoes to beat yo' ass and murder you in broad daylight. Brock thought he could betray the Taleo name and still be associated with us and the INC? Nah. The INC is sacred—my Pop was one of its founding fathers. He and his frat brothers had to find ways to help their families and take their Cartels to higher heights. After a great deal of planning and meetings, the INC was born. So, betraying us meant betraying them, and that's something I'd never allow to happen. I'd always stand in the gap for my Pop and the other founding fathers, at all costs. I lived for the INC, and I'd proudly die for it too.

"Nigga, we really gon' sit here and watch these niggas snore? I distribute yo' pappy's drugs; I'm not yo' assistant to murdering a nigga. That's what you got cat woman ass for. Da fuck!" Mace whispered as he fussed, and I swear I wanted to knock his ass on the bed with them.

Milan eased into the room. Standing at 5'8", Milan was a pure chocolate beauty with curves that could stop traffic and have any nigga drop to his knees in admiration. She had long, flowing hair that she usually kept up in a ponytail, giving her straight China doll vibes. She was beautiful; I couldn't deny the truth. I was a married man in love with my wife, but facts are facts. When I first met her, I was definitely caught up on her beauty. Later, I found out we were both playing for the same damn team, and all I could do was shake my damn head and laugh. Milan's skills and beauty made her an extremely deadly weapon, and it'd been an advantage that we capitalized on every single time.

Dressed in a black body suit, she eased by the bed, nudging her gun on the side of Brock's head, causing his eyes to pop open. Looking around like he'd seen a ghost, he didn't make a single move. With tears streaming down his face, he knew what it was as he watched Jakari stand with his gun pointed at him. Mace walked over to the bed to tie his hands. He knew not to move, and if he did, Milan would snap his neck. His weight didn't matter; she was skilled and trained to take you out by any means necessary.

Minutes later, she was climbing on to the bed. Her movements were slick with ease...calm and deliberate. That action was short-lived because no sooner than her knee pressed into the mattress, Brock's wife was waking up. I guess she felt that something was off because her eyes opened and closed. She was trying to focus, but the sounds of her husband heavily hyperventilating caused her to turn in his direction quickly. Milan was sitting on the damn pillow near his head like her ass was a part of the pillow sham.

"Oh fuck! What the hell are y'all doing in our house?!" Blanca shouted, immediately trying to jump up and go for her gun.

At least she had heart, more heart than her bitch of a husband had. I cleared my throat, and her ass instantly froze, turning to face me with tears filling her eyes. She tried to fix her posture and make movements with her naked body. I chuckled because none of that shit phased me, and pussy damn sure doesn't move me. It was crazy how she thought her looks would save her. She was indeed beautiful, but it was that plastic surgery kind of beauty, and I was cool on that. I loved my women natural, and if she had some extra love handles, that was even better. A nigga like me needed something to hold on to, to love on a little better, so Blanca's good looks wouldn't earn her any points here. I'd seen beautiful women my entire life, and before marrying

6

the most beautiful woman in the world, I'd sampled more than a few.

I nodded in Milan's direction, and she eased behind Blanca, gripping her neck, and snapped her shit, right before sending a single slug to her head for good measure. Brain matter splattered all over the bed, and this bitch nigga cried out for his wife but still didn't make a move.

"Damn, nigga kick or somethin'!" Kari spat. I chuckled because I felt the same way. Try to put up some type of fight for what's yours. Trust me, when it came to mine, you gon' have to take me first 'cause bitch it's up!

If you looked up the word pussy in the dictionary, this nigga Brock's picture would be the definition. His girl only got that easy kill 'cause at least she made an attempt to fight for her life. I mean, she would've never won that shit, but she tried. Brock's screams after seeing his wife's lifeless body did nothing but fuel my anger. Because this nigga was a bitch! I hate a pussy nigga, damn!

He continued to scream, cry, and beg for mercy and all I could think about was emptying my clip in this nigga throat. Just to shut him the fuck up! But we'd promised Milan we wouldn't interfere, so I did my best to keep my word.

"Man, watching this nigga stomach do all that damn shaking as he exhales is fuckin' disturbing. Put this nigga out his misery. All that belly shaking making me damn dizzy. Nigga, you over here crying for her ass, and she was trying to throw the pussy at my homie. It's too early for this shit. I started to decline yo' shit, Jav. You really be taking this friend-ship shit too far. I'ma make sure I don't answer shit else from you muthafuckas until noon. It shouldn't be shit going on until then."

"Please, Javari! Don't do this shit. It's not what you think. They threatened to kill my mom and wife if I didn't side with them. I know Uncle Vincent didn't approve of this shit. He loves us too much to approve of this," Brock whimpered.

He knew me and damn sure knew Milan. He'd seen her work. So, he already knew this wasn't a polite visit; it was indeed his death sentence. Jakari and I normally wouldn't be here, but this shit was personal to us since we trusted this pussy ass nigga. I wanted to be the last muthafucka he saw before he took his last breath. Then he would know not to cross the Taleo's, even in hell! I stood and walked over to the bed with my gun, tapping that shit hard as fuck on his forehead.

"Nigga, fuck you, yo bitch, and yo' muthafuckin' mama! Did you think about yo' mama when you walked your fat, sloppy, funky ass to the side of betrayal? You knew the moment you made that decision and listened to this dead bitch, that it was a wrap for all of you. My Pop wants you dead, I want you dead, and my brother wants you dead! So, guess what?

Nigga, you DEAD! The fuck! The rules were simple. Loyalty keeps you alive, and disloyalty puts you in the dirt! Well, in your case, the fire 'cause you know what it means when a Taleo kills you. I'ma burn yo' bitch ass and send your ashes to yo' mama, so she can put you in a necklace, nigga! Milan is here to make that shit a reality." I pulled my gun away from his head.

"Damn! That whole speech scared the fuck outta me! Especially, that nigga you dead part." Mace dumb ass shrugged, shaking his head, and Kari burst into laughter. He was right; I should've left his unserious ass home.

"Nooo! Fuck nooo! Javari, pleaseee! Man, don't do this. I'll do whatever I have to do!" he pleaded, and I'd heard enough. I nodded and walked back to take my seat in the corner of the room while Milan did what she did best.

Easing out her famous mask, Brock finally squirmed, trying to stop Milan from putting it on his face. Once she got it on successfully, she pressed the button, and it had to be about fifty tiny needles that sprouted out and injected his face with a drug that slowly stopped your motor functions. It would ultimately shut down your vital organs, but it was done slowly. Eventually, he'd stop moving. His teary eyes danced around the room trying to stay focused, but he knew he was dying. Milan eased out her knife and began placing tiny cuts into his face, arms, and legs. Blood was seeping out of him, and his screams were crucial as the tears poured out of his eyes.

Milan got off of the bed, grabbed the acid she'd brought in with her, and started to pour it all over his face, and as she poured it, it ate through his skin. His muffled screams sounded more like a gargle and the scene was gruesome. She repeated the process until his gurgling ceased, which let us know that his heart had stopped beating. I wanted that nigga to feel every ounce of his death, and she made sure of it. His death was slow, extreme, and deliberate. It was torture at its best.

"Once they come pick them up, we need to go back to your house so the chef can cook me a burger. Killing these snake muthafuckas got me hungry." Milan smiled, and I shook my head fast as shit cause hell no.

"A burger! You just had brain splatter all over yo' top lip and yo' hard stomach ass wanna go eat a burger. Lan, you need to go sit on somebody couch 'cause I'm convinced yo' ass was hurt as a child. You need to let that aggression out, witcho crazy ass." Mace ass looked from Milan to the dead niggas she'd just killed. His ass didn't care what came out of his mouth.

"Nah, take that shit to Jakari's Crib." I chuckled at the thought, but it wasn't happening.

I knew my wife wouldn't be on that type of time. She didn't care for Milan, and Milan damn sure wasn't fond of her. Tori always thought that Milan wanted me and her being gay was just a front. I tried to assure her that there was nothing she had to worry about and it wasn't like that with Milan. Tori has always been very vocal about her dislike of Milan and how she didn't believe shit she had to say. She even tried to flex her hand as my wife and tried to get me to fire her. It didn't work like that; my dad ran this family and he said who was fired and hired. Besides that, he loved himself some Milan.

"Mace is right; your stomach hard as fuck. I wouldn't be able to eat after burning a nigga alive with acid." I chuckled. This girl didn't play about her food, but I wouldn't be able to do it after the shit that just went down in here.

"Doesn't bother me." She shrugged, walking into their bathroom to take a shower. How you gon' kill these folk in their shit and then go use their shower to wash it the fuck off? Milan was straight gangsta with that shit.

"Lan is diabolical for that move." Jakari shook his head while pointing in the direction of the bathroom, and I burst into laughter.

"I know you fuckin' lyin'! 'Cause how you gon' take your murderous ass in these people bathroom and wash their blood off you? Blood that you caused because you killed these niggas. If I was this dead bitch, I would rise from the dead and drown yo' ass." Mace shook his head, and we all fell out laughing. One thing for sure, Milan stressed him the fuck out.

Mace and I have been friends since high school. He was having this big birthday bash, and for weeks he had been talking about a friend of his that he grew up with that he wanted me to meet. He said they had lost touch for a while, but he ran back into her on some business shit. Mace wasn't just my best friend; he was also the head of all of Taleo's distribution. His opinion meant everything to me, and I trusted him. He knew that we were looking for a hitta and thought that she would be a good asset to the family. My Pop was indeed the head of our family and Cartel, but I was second in command. So, if she wanted a job with us, she would have to come through me.

When I first laid eyes on Milan, I couldn't believe that she was an assassin. It was indeed a job that she would have to prove to me that she could do. We clicked that night; I was really intrigued by her intelligence and beauty. After we spoke for a few, I was definitely interested to hear about her career choice. Even though I was interested in her, she also had me ready to end her fuckin' life, and that's some real shit. I shook my head just thinking about the way things went down.

"It's nice to meet you, Milan," I said, intrigued by our conversation. "I'm interested in what you can do, but I'm not the type to take anyone's word for it. You'll have to show me. Maybe I'll tag along on your next job and teach you a thing or two. I've mastered this game." I winked.

She smirked. "I love teachable moments, Javari. Keep your head on a swivel. My show-don't-tell moment might come sooner than you think." She stood, extended her hand, and I pulled it to my lips, kissing it lightly. She chuckled and strutted off, leaving me stuck.

A few nights later, I was knocked the fuck out in bed with my wife, Tori, while my one-year-old daughter, Ciani, slept peacefully in her bedroom across the hall. The house was locked down as usual, with security in place. Suddenly, I felt a soft touch on my face, followed by Ciani's giggles.

"Tori, Ciani's out of bed," I grumbled, nudging her to get up. When she didn't respond, I opened my eyes because my daughter was only one and supposed to have been in her crib. There was no way she could get out. I almost lost my shit, seeing Milan standing over me with a smile, holding my daughter in her arms.

This crazy muthafucka had gotten into my house, past all my guards. Not to mention, she broke through my top of the line security system that secured my compound. I immediately reached under my pillow for my gun, but it wasn't there. Milan smiled, placing the gun down on my nightstand, and twisted out of my bedroom with my daughter in her arms. I jumped up, mad as fuck with murder on my mind.

Throwing on a pair of sweats and grabbing my gun, I rushed out of my room to see her walking out of Ciani's bedroom. I wasted no time putting my gun to her head, and at the same time, she smoothly put a needle to my neck.

"We can die together," she said calmly. "Or you can take this as a lesson. Your family could've been gone tonight. I'm here because I want to work for you. You're the hardest man to get next to, and I needed to prove that I could. Consider this my resume. This is my teachable moment...That show and not tell moment you spoke of." She gave a slight smile, and my trigger finger started involuntarily jerking.

I was on fuckin' fire!

*"Get the fuck out!" I gritted in her face. I was so damn close to her I could've bit her fuckin' lips off her face and spit them muthafuckas back at her.*

*Fuck that teachable moment shit and her fuckin' resume! Once I put her ass out, I fired every guard I had on the grounds.*

*A few days later, my twin brother, Jakari, and I watched the surveillance footage. Milan had taken out my security system and climbed the walls like she was cat woman around this muthafucka. It was impressive...Intriguing to say the least.*

*After some thought about it and convincing from Jakari, I hired her a few days later. From that moment on, she was hired as our top assassin for the Taleo Cartel, and we'd been friends ever since. Despite her breaking into my shit, we hit it off instantly, and as time went by, she proved to be as solid as they came. That was my hitta for sure, and I trusted her with my life. Trust me, if she was ever in a situation, just know I was coming, and I wanted all the smoke when it came to her.*

"Javari...Jav!" Jakari's voice jolted me out of my thoughts. "The crew is here, let's go." He walked out of the room, and I stood from my seat to follow him out.

Our cleanup crew wasted no time getting to work, cleaning up the mess we'd made, and wrapping the bodies to send back to our spot for cremation. Once that was complete, their ashes would be packed and shipped. Yeah, I'ma petty nigga. I'd kill you, burn yo' ass, then send the remains to your people with my deepest regards. It's a deep and twisted kind of way, but it was my way. We owned our own funeral home, but it was strictly for our personal shit. No grieving families, no tearful goodbyes. Just dead niggas, ashes and closure, served our fuckin' way. If you asked me, it was some admirable shit. At least we send you back to your folks.

"What you got planned for the day?" I asked my brother as we stepped outside.

"Not much," Jakari said with a shrug. "Gotta go over some security plans for Pop's travel to Tokyo." Kari was the man behind all of our security. "Other than that, I'm chillin' until tonight. Milan talked me into going to this party with her and Mace."

I stopped and gave him a side-eye. "You? A party? With them?"

He laughed. "Man, you already know what it is with them. It's always a time." He wasn't lying though. The Milan we knew off the clock was nothing like her on the clock. She was a fool, greedy, and loved fuckin' with Mace.

I laughed, but for some reason, I was a little on edge. They asses always got into some shit when they were out and knowing that made me nervous. Jakari was my twin brother, a duplicate of myself. Our hazel eyes shifted to green depending on our mood or the colors we wore. We had sleek noses, full lips, muscular builds, and many tattoos that covered our bodies. The shit scared me sometimes, because looking at him seemed like I was looking in the mirror. Everything about us was a carbon copy, from our looks to our

15

demeanor. We got our caramel-brown complexion, and attitude from our Pop, but the rest, that was all Camille Taleo.

Our mom stamped her looks onto us from the womb. Every time we stepped into a room, women threw themselves at us. That shit annoyed the fuck outta my wife, Tori. She hated the way women flocked around us, but there wasn't much I could do about it. It's just how we moved, but I would never allow someone to disrespect her, nor would I do that shit. My wife was my life, and the day she gave me my daughter only heightened my love for her.

Jakari and I shared a bond that went deeper than blood. Born eight minutes apart, I took my role as the big brother seriously. Protecting him was second nature. We also had that twin intuition thing going for us where we knew what the other one was thinking without even having to say much. Often, we'd even finish each other's sentences, and we damn sure knew when something was wrong with the other one.

There wasn't much different about us besides Jakari being the brainiac between us. He was a tech wizard who could find anyone, anywhere. You could be hiding in some back alley in Bangkok, and he'd still pull your location like it was nothing. He was smart as shit, and him being the computer geek that he was gave us an advantage over the Cartels. I mean, I'm sure they had their techs, but nothing like what Kari could do over here.

"Don't get into too much shit tonight," I told him, shaking my head.

Jakari smiled. "Now you know that's not my thing. I'll be good."

Yeah, right. With Milan and Mace in the mix, 'Good' wasn't even apart of their damn vocabulary. My brother wasn't like me. He didn't want to be too deep in this Cartel shit. Don't get me wrong, he would bust his guns with the best of us and would damn sure put your ass in the death rate toll. But the background is where he wanted to be. So, I wasn't putting shit past him when Milan's crazy ass was involved.

After dapping him up, I headed home to fuck new life into my wife. By the time I made it back home, my family was awake. Ciani was in the kitchen with her nanny having break-fast, so I took that as my key to slide inside of my wife real quick. Walking into the bedroom, she was just coming out of the shower with a white towel wrapped around her. I wasted no time removing my clothes and pulling the towel off of her.

"Good morning, beautiful," I spoke between kisses as one hand caressed her breast and the other eased down to her pussy.

"Fuck!" She moaned as my fingers brushed over her clit. The moment my fingers entered her folds, her body started trembling, and the more I massaged her clit, the worse she got. Tori couldn't hang for shit, but my wife had the best pussy a nigga could've asked for. She tried grabbing my dick and I smacked her hand away.

"Don't touch my shit." I smiled, gently pushing her back

on the bed, spreading her legs apart and diving in. Sucking, slurping, and nibbling on the pussy so good baby girl was talking in tongues.

"Javari, I can't take it. Please give me the dick." She begged, and I obliged. Hovering over her, I started massaging my dick on her clit before easing inside of her.

"Ahhhh shit!" she tried her best to take the dick, but she kept pushing my stomach, trying to get me to ease up. We went through this shit every time, and she knew that wasn't happening. We had a safe word. If she said it, then I would back off, but that word isn't really used unless she's in some type of pain.

"Fuck!" I growled, pounding the fuck out of her as she clenched her pussy muscles around my dick. That shit always did something to me. It caused me to go harder, and all she could do was hold on. When it came to the shit between my legs, I was a fuckin' problem, and that lil nigga will have you screaming and creaming every fucking time.

"Mmmm! Shitttt!" she moaned.

"Got damn, baby girl! This some good pussy!" I growled, crashing my lips onto hers. For the next hour, we went at it, and I didn't let up until I got my fill of her.

---

AN OVERWHELMING FEELING washed over me as I sped through the city at top speed in my Lambo with my wife on the passenger side. We were on our way home. I wanted to do something nice for her, so we had an impromptu date night. I didn't often get an opportunity to have those moments with her, so any time we had an opportunity, I tried to take them. Tori was the love of my life. I met her in my senior year in college, and from that day on, she's been mine. Once I locked in on you, that's that. You're mine whether you like that shit or not. She gave me a hard time at first, but eventually, she did the right thing. A few minutes later, we were pulling up to our security key pad so that it could scan my car and open the gates.

"It's still early. Are you staying in tonight?" Tori lightly rubbed her finger across my hand. As much as I wanted to stay in with her, that overwhelming feeling rushed over me again, and my mind flashed to Jakari, Mace, and Milan.

"Nah, I need to make a run and check on my brother. I won't be long, thou—" My ringing phone interrupted me, and I saw that it was Milan.

I immediately answered. "Yeah."

"The Sandoval's are in the club, and Ziek is already on his shit. Telling Jakari they have unfinished business from the night of the Monster's Ball. Kari is on ten. We tried to get him to leave but yeah, he's not listening. I think you need to get down here. You can consider Ziek a dead man walking though." Milan ended the call, and the moment I looked over at Tori, she was sucking her damn teeth.

When the car came to a stop, she hopped out, and I let

out a deep breath because I knew she was about to be on some bullshit. Me and Tori had been together for six years, and she'd been down for me through it all, and I loved her for that shit. It was hard to find someone that loves you for you and not for what you could give them. So for that, I'd give her the world. She just needed to calm down on this attitude shit she'd been on.

I got out of the car and followed her inside because one thing I hated was for my woman to be upset with something concerning me. I had to fix my home before things went too far. If my mental state wasn't right, shit could go left real quick. If I was feeling fucked up that made things around me fucked up. Everybody might die based off an attitude that stemmed from my wife, and I couldn't have that shit.

"Tori, why do we have to keep going through this shit? What's the attitude for? I've always kept shit a hundred with you. You know what I'm into, and the things that you don't know about are for your protection and the protection of my family. My Pop is talking about stepping down in the next few years, and if he does, I'm stepping into his spot. That's something we've discussed because my brother doesn't want to be in that position. If that happens, things will get more complex with me, and I'll be gone a lot more.

Being away from you and Ciani isn't what I want, but to keep you in this house and to give you the lavish life you live for. And let's not mistake this shit. You live for it; my bank account and credit cards tell me daily. I just need for you to trust that when I'm not with you, I'm doing right by you. It's some shit going on with my brother, and I need to go check on him."

"Why do you do that shit, Jav?! Jakari is a big boy, and he can handle his own shit. Can't we have a night out and you not have to run out as soon as we get home? It's always like this! It never fucking ends!" She spat, sucking her teeth with an attitude.

"Lil mama, I need for you to bring that down a notch. I just sat here and explained everything to you. You're not going to sit here and act like we don't spend time together; that'll never be the case. When I'm out with you, or home spending time, all of my time and attention is on you. It's always been like that and always will be, so don't act like you don't get enough of me. Even though what I do is complex, I still make sure you know that you and Ciani are the most important people in my life. I'll drop anything that I'm doing when you call and say you need me, and you know that. Right now, my family needs me," I said to her as she walked inside of our bar lounge to pour herself a drink.

"Maybe what you're doing isn't enough anymore, Jav! Maybe I want more of you and from you! Any nigga would be glad to have a woman like me on his arm. Don't push me in that direction." She let that shit slip off her tongue as easily as that brown eased down her throat. Placing my gun on the bar, I turned her to face me with my hand wrapped around her throat, stopping the liquor from its path down.

21

"I have never disrespected you. EVER! I've given you the best part of me and never given you a reason to doubt my love for you. Applying pressure around your neck to stop your muthafuckin' air supply isn't something I do to my woman. But let this moment be a reminder to you when you decide you want to disrespect me by saying some shit like that. As much as I love you, I fuckin' love me more, and I'll never knowingly let you play in my muthafuckin' face! NEVER!

Now if you cherish this marriage and your fuckin' life, make that the last time you spit some stupid shit like that out of your mouth." I turned her loose and her ass was coughing for dear life. I left her right there, gasping and rubbing her neck.

This goes right back to that LOYALTY word. Her lack of understanding and how easily she threw another nigga up in my face, had me looking at her sideways. I loved my wife with everything in me, but telling me that she was going to get another nigga was some next level courage. Especially telling an unstable nigga like me some shit like that. I'll have both of their asses dangling from the Ben Franklin Bridge. Tori wasn't exempt from showing loyalty. If anything, I held her ass to a higher standard than these other muthafuckas. She didn't even realize how quickly she almost lost her life and left our daughter motherless.

I rushed out of my house and headed towards Vault with my mind on a thousand. Truthfully, I hated when me and

Tori got into it, because it fucked my head up, and a nigga like me needed to always be on point.

It took me about twenty minutes to pull up to Vault and just as I got out, people were already running out of the club. I didn't have to wonder why after that call I got from Milan because one thing about my brother, his temper was like mine —deadly. The club was dark inside as the fluorescent lights flashed and Lil Baby floated through the speakers. Despite whatever had popped off, it still was shoulder to shoulder packed, so I had to push my way through the crowd with my gun on my side while scanning the club for their section.

Just as I made my way into VIP, Kari was going toe to toe with Ziek. With the loud music blaring, I couldn't hear shit they were saying, but I could tell by the grimace on my twin's face, whatever Ziek was saying had him plexed up. Before I knew it, Ziek had pulled his gun, and before he had a chance to fire, it Kari had let off a shot to his head. This club wasn't a club that we had control over, so I had to get him out of here. ASAP! As soon as the shots rang out, everything got chaotic. People were pushing and shoving their way towards the exit while I was heading in the opposite direction and trying to get to my twin.

"Give me your gun, Jakari! Mace, y'all get him out of here!" I demanded.

"Jav!" Jakari looked at me, not trying to make a move. I needed to try and get him out of here, before it was too late, so I snatched the gun out of his hands and pushed him towards the VIP exit. There were too many witnesses around, which left him vulnerable.

"Get out of here!" I roared.

"Hands up!" Club security had me surrounded. I had to think quickly because this was just the club's security, not the cops. This was one of those times that I hated that I didn't have my security detail with me. Luckily, I was the only one still standing over Ziek's lifeless body, and my brother was a few feet away, so security had only seen me. Both of us being locked up wouldn't have been any good for either of us. Glaring at my brother, Milan, and Mace still standing stuck, I grimaced.

"Now!" I shouted, and Mace pulled Jakari and Milan away while I was left to deal with this murder charge I was about to be hit with.

*Fuckkkkkkk!*

Minutes later, the Philadelphia Police Department was surrounding me and flooded the entire VIP area. These muthafuckas was about to have a field day once they learned who I was. The Feds were trying everything in their power to get something on the Taleo's, and this was going to be a shit show for sure. I knew we should've handled these niggas the night of the Monster's Ball. Allowing them to breathe after that disrespect should've never happened, and it was all over a bitch.

The Monster's Ball was an event that we all lived for. In this Cartel life, it was a party that we looked forward to every year. It was the who's who event where members of the INC came together to break bread and party like only they could. It wasn't just a party though. It was indeed a sacred meeting of power and legacy created by the founding fathers of the INC. The only way an outside Cartel could step foot inside the ball was if they were a plus one by a founding family. Other than that, there was no way to get inside. It was for us, by us, to celebrate us. Now, here I was in a position where I was unprotected, cuffed, and about to be hit with a murder charge.

I sent my brother out of here because I wanted to get a handle on this shit. Never did I expect to get caught up like this. Not over this pussy ass nigga Ziek Sandoval. Fuckkkkk!

Hearing them read me my rights went in one ear and out the other because thoughts of my family, my wife, and daughter rushed me and hit like a ton of bricks. I knew they would be taken care of, but being taken away from them didn't sit right with me. My mind drifted to the night of the ball, where all this bullshit happened.

*"Pop texted and said that he was already here,"* I said to Jakari as we walked up to the entrance of the mansion. Kari, Tori and I were running late, so our Pop went on without us. These events weren't my mom's thing, so she never came, and tonight was no different.

*"Names and Password?"* The guard questioned.

*"Javari Taleo, Jakari Taleo, and my guest, Latoria Taleo. The password is, Year of the Mafia."*

25

"Enjoy your night. The Taleo's are at section seven." Once we were done with the guard, we headed to the section he said we were in. I saw the founding families were all in attendance. The DaVinche Cartel and The Belaire Cartel were across from us, but it didn't look as if all of the Belaire Cartel was here yet. It's been a minute, so I had to make time to see what's up with them.

"Hey, Jakari." This chick Asia spoke. I saw her on the arms of Ziek Sandoval, and I knew that nigga was about to be on some bullshit.

I knew he was going to be here because the Hundero Cartel invited him. My dad invited our cousins, the Black Brothers, because they were making a lot of noise in the streets and moving a lot of guns through several territories, so their connections and reach was long. Besides that, they were my mother's nephews and we would always look out for them. I was cool with the Black's, but that nigga Ziek could get these hollow tips any day. I hated that nigga! It was nothing new that the Taleo's didn't like the Sandoval's and Ziek was the head of that Cartel because his father stepped down. It was like he lived to try his hand with me and Jakari, and the only reason that he was still amongst the living was because my Pop didn't want us to touch him. He didn't like his ass either, but we couldn't touch him. Make that shit make sense because me and my damn Glock don't understand it.

"Sup, shorty." Kari nodded his head as he poured himself a drink.

"Jakari, I would love to get to know you better." She smiled, taking a seat next to Kari uninvited.

"Nah, I'm good. Aren't you here with the dude Ziek? Ion play them games, lil mama. If you with that man, go be with him. I'd hate for this to get deadly because you're being messy. The fuck out my face!" Kari stood on his business and didn't give not one fuck.

That's what I loved about my brother. He was on some computer tech shit, but he stood ten toes down for his respect, family, and business. My baby brother busted them guns when he needed to. She got her ass up and ran off back to where she came from. I was looking at some of the other sections, and some of the other cartels hadn't arrived yet. About an hour later, champagne was being poured, and everyone raised their glasses and recited our oath.

"To the INC! To the INC! To the INC!" We chanted. "I stand on the foundation of our codes. I give my loyalty and pledge to protect all things that bind us together. I will honor my brothers and stand on the shoulders of our Allegiance. No disloyalty, insubordination, or perfidy will be tolerated. I accept any consequences for those acts. Flesh of my Flesh. Blood of my Blood. I give my life for the INC and I'll die for the INC." Once we were finished, we drank our champagne and went back to enjoying the night.

"So, nigga, you threatened my fucking girl!" Ziek rushed into our section and up in Jakari's face, which was the wrong decision because Kari wasted no time jumping on his ass!

27

*He was beating the shit out of this dude, and I sat down and enjoyed the bloody show. Kari was throwing blow after blow, not giving Ziek enough time to even get a punch in. My Pop and security rushed over, breaking the fight up. Ziek was damn near unconscious, and his lying ass girl ran up screaming in Kari's face. That was short-lived because Milan came out of nowhere and ate her ass for dinner. It was all out of control, so I stood up to get some order with my camp. We definitely didn't want to seem like the unhinged, unprofessional ones. But yeah, don't ever try us, especially over some petty ass mess like that. It was childish and so beneath us. That's some shit these street niggas, and corner boys are into. Not on the levels we're on, we shouldn't be in an elite event like this fighting over a bitch that didn't even belong to us.*

*"Let's go now!" My Pop yelled, and we followed him out. I was sure this lil' problem wasn't over.*

"Javari Taleo! What have you gotten yourself into?" Agent Diaz questioned with a smirk, jolting me out of my thoughts.

Seeing him here on the scene, I knew I was going to have a long battle ahead. This nigga hated my family, and he hated me even more. But ain't nothing bitch about me, not even when it came to these Fed muthafuckas.

"I'm only talking to my lawyer." Is all I had to say. Then they pulled me out of the club and placed me into the back of a patrol car to get me out of there. I'd make the call to my Pop once I got situated. I knew we had judges, local police, and

Feds on our payroll and with some protection from the INC, I was hoping that I didn't have to sit long.

---

### Three Days Later

"I WANT YOU HOME, Javari! Why the hell would you take the fall for something you didn't do?" Tori cried, her voice trembling with anger and fear. I understood her frustration— her world was unraveling, and I was the cause of it. But no matter how much it hurt, there was no way I could anyone else, know the truth. Jakari was the one who took out Ziek, and I'd be damned if I let my little brother take the fall.

Neither of us intended for this to happen, but if I could do it all over again, I would do that shit the same fuckin' way. I was going to get home to my wife and child if that was the last thing I did. That was a promise. It'd taken a lot of convincing and having Jakari followed by our security detail for him not to turn himself in. He'd tried several times, and that wasn't the move.

"I know, baby. I'm trying to figure it all out so that I can get back to you and Ciani. I'll be home soon, I promise. I gotta go. I'll see you when I get to court. Remember, whatever happens, never let them see you break." We said our goodbyes then ended the call.

I was praying that Jakari wouldn't get out of hand in court

today. My lawyer said that they might not give me bail. Hearing that took everything to keep him from turning himself in. He'd tried to confess before and Pop had to double down on his security detail. I knew my brother was built for this, but I'ma get out of this. Pop was doing everything he could with the connections we had, but shit wasn't moving as fast as we'd hoped it would. The FBI was all over my ass with this case, and Agent Diaz wanted to make sure I went down. I made a mental note to have Milan pay him a visit as soon as possible.

I got locked up on Friday night, so I had to sit over the weekend. I knew I was going to court today; I just didn't know what time I would be leaving. About an hour later, the officer walked up to my cell, and I was escorted out so that I could go to my bail hearing. The guards ushered me into the courtroom with shackles on my feet and cuffs on my hands. I felt like a caged animal, and that shit was fucking with me. Giving a warm smile to my family, I took a seat beside my attorney.

I was kind of hopeful, but that shit went right out the window when the prosecutor started talking. This nigga was so relentless you would've thought that I wiped out this man's entire family. He painted me as a threat to society, while my lawyer fought just as hard for them to allow me to have a bond. After a long deliberation, the judge leaned forward and looked directly over at me.

"Bail denied! Trial is set for September 3rd." The gavel slammed, and that sound rang out in my ears.

It was final. I sat frozen in place. The courtroom erupted with cheers from bystanders and screams of sadness from my family. *September*. Damn, that was far as fuck. Damn near six months away.

"Wait! Nooo! What the hell do they mean bail is denied? I thought he would get a bail!" My wife screamed in anger, looking from me to my Pop.

"This is your fault, and you better own up to your shit!" Tori jumped into Jakari's face.

"Tori, let it go! I'm good. I need y'all to stay strong. I got this shit. Kari, I got this, bro. Come see me soon. Tori, I love you, baby. Kiss my baby girl for me." She watched as they pulled me out of the courtroom.

Pop nodded in my direction to let me know that he was working on it. I trusted my father, and I knew he was working day in and out to get me out of this shit. That alone lets a nigga rest easy.

JAVARI

### Six Months Later

SIX MONTHS, that's how long I'd been behind these walls. I'd literally been through every emotion imaginable as I sat and waited for this day. Anger, distress, guilt, and promise washed over me daily. I was relieved that the day was finally here, but I'm not gon' lie; that shit was hard as fuck. I kept thinking about this moment, so I tossed and turned all night and didn't get much sleep. This was the day that would determine the rest of my life. My charges were heavy, and I had the weight of the world on my shoulders.

Nothing was pussy about me. Heavy or not, I was holding this time down. I just wished that I would've thought this through a little more. Especially with the fact that we were in unchartered territory with the club. Kari said that the club owner was friends with Ziek, and as soon as they got outside, he ran to grab his laptop and tapped into the club's camera feed. He was on point with that. I'm just hoping my attorney can get some of these charges dropped. I knew he had a meeting with the prosecution and prayed everything worked out in my favor.

My mind ventured to my wife and daughter. I missed the hell out of my family. Tori, with her quick-tempered ass, was pissed with me. I could understand her anger just a little. If I could've had this shit any other way, getting hemmed up wouldn't be my option. When it comes to Jakari and his temper, we were one in the same in a sense. Once we're up, it's hard to come down. The difference with us is Kari doesn't stop unless you stop him and I'm about the only one who can stop him. He's a quiet storm; it can take a while for him to get there, but he'll try to ignore conflict at all costs. I was different in that way. I welcomed the bullshit because I'ma damn sure end it my way. I promised my mom that I would always protect my brother. I stand on that promise because my guy really doesn't bother anybody. He's always in his own world, coming up with new ways to protect and guard his family.

I tried to explain my position to my wife, but she didn't care. In fact, she expressed how she really felt about my family. Screaming on the phone that she hated my brother and that he was the reason I was behind bars when in reality, I'm the reason I'm behind these damn walls! I stepped in, grabbed his gun, and made them leave. If it was up to Kari, he would be sitting here right now, not me.

One minute Tori confesses how much she loves me, and then she's talking about divorcing me and taking our daughter.

Her emotions were back and forth daily. I've apologized to her for the way things are because she deserves that. But all that divorcing me and taking my daughter was out the window. The fuck she thought she was talking to! I missed the fuck out of her and my daughter. I haven't seen Ciani in months, because the first time she brought her up here, she was asking questions as to why I was here. Ci-Ci is seven years old. I didn't want my child to see me like this, like some damn caged animal in cuffs.

"Taleo!" Hearing the guard's voice jolted me back to reality. He approached my cell, and I stood quietly, waiting for him to secure the restraints before ushering me out of my cell.

An hour later, I was sitting in a holding room at the courthouse. I was on edge and felt like the damn walls were closing in on me. As strong as I am, this shit was still wearing down on me. I would never let a muthafucka see me sweat, but when I'm alone, my mind wanders. The door opened, and my attorney, Lance Robinson, came walking into the room with his briefcase strapped across his shoulder, a file under his arm, and determination on his face. He seemed ready, at least I hope he was.

"It's good to see you, Mr. Taleo," he greeted me with a handshake and took a seat next to me. "I know today is weighing heavy on you. I spoke to your father, and he expressed his concerns about you being behind bars. I'm doing everything I possibly can to get you home to your family." He sighed as he scanned pages in his folder.

"Thank you for working so diligently to get me out of here." I gave him a half smile because there truly wasn't shit to smile about. I was in some deep shit.

"I have some good and bad news, unfortunately. I met with the prosecution this morning hoping he would be willing to drop some of these charges. He agreed to withdraw the gun charge. Even though the gun was registered to you, it was clean, and you have the right to purchase a firearm through a private seller when you're licensed to carry." Nodding, I sat back and listened to him intently without saying a word so that he could continue.

"I was able to get the murder charge reduced to voluntary manslaughter, and that's a win for us because you would've been facing life without the possibility of parole. It seems that they couldn't produce the video surveillance from the club. With that being said, if they have no video, we have an argument. We have witnesses that are willing to testify that Ziek was the aggressor. That he pulled his gun on you, and that you acted in self-defense." He sat back, allowing me to take in everything that he'd just said.

"Do you feel that you've done all that you can to get these charges reduced?" I questioned.

"Yes, that's the best we can do under these circumstances," he stated, and I stood from my seat.

"Then I appreciate your help, and I know that you'll fight for me in that courtroom. Let's go get this show on the road.

I'm prepared to either sit or go home. My positive thinking is for me to go home." I shrugged.

"Let's look on the brighter side of things just for today." Lance smiled as he knocked on the door to let the guard know that we were ready to go.

"I'm not a dude that's one sided. I look at things from different angles. When I'm in a dark place, there was nothing, and I mean, nothing bright about that shit. The Feds and even some local police had been trying to get at us for the longest. Now that they have one of us, so I was sure they'll try to pin everything they can on me." I looked over at him, and he nodded in understanding. All I wanted from him was that he put up a fight for me as if he were fighting for his own life. So far, he was doing just that.

A few hours had passed and the attorneys on both sides had been fighting tooth and nail. My entire family sat behind me in the courtroom, filled with emotions. My mom sat with tears in her eyes and all I wanted to do was wrap my arms around her. There is no love like a mother's love, and as hard as I am, my mom was still my blanket of comfort. My pop, brother, and Mace sat stoned-faced, and I knew they were holding it all in. Even Milan sat with my family with tears in her eyes, but what tripped me out was that my wife sat scrolling on her phone with a blank expression. She didn't seem to give a damn about what was going on around her. Like my fuckin' life wasn't on the line!

FIVE DAYS HAVE PASSED, and the attorneys did their closing arguments yesterday. The Jury was currently in deliberations, and we weren't sure how long that would take. I believe that my attorney went in and gave it all he had. We were walking into the courtroom because the Jury had finally reached a verdict, and no lie, I was a ball of nerves.

"The honorable Jeffery Andrews presiding," the court guard called out as the judge walked in and took his seat. Minutes later, the jury was walking in.

"Will the defendant rise?" The judge spoke and looked over at the jury. "Jury foreman, have you reached your verdict?" He questioned.

"Yes, sir we have." He passed the card over to the guard and he passed it to the judge. His expression was unreadable.

"What's your verdict?"

"On the count of Voluntary Manslaughter, we find the defendant... *Guilty!*"

The courtroom erupted into madness. Emotions filled the room, drowning out my own thoughts of what I just heard.

"Mr. Taleo," the judge called out over the noise. "You've been found guilty of Voluntary Manslaughter. I don't think there's any reason to delay sentencing. I hereby sentence you to twenty years without the possibility of parole."

I stood numb. I heard what he said, but my words barely

registered. *Twenty fuckin' years!* My chest felt tight, but I'd never show signs of weakness.

"Oh, my God! Nooo! Vincent, you gotta do something! Get my son out of this, Vincent!" My mother's cries nearly broke me.

"Nah, hell no! I'm not letting that shit slide! It wasn't him!" Jakari's voice cut through the air, and that snapped me back to reality.

"Jakariii!" I roared, commanding the room, and everything in it stood still. "I got this. You just take care of them. I'll find a way out of this."

"Twenty years. What the fuck am I supposed to do with that verdict, Jav? I hope you don't think that I'ma wait on you for twenty years. I love you, but that's not happening!" My wife shouted, and there really wasn't much I could say to her.

"I'm sorry, Tori. I'm apologizing to you again because my apology to you needs to be just as big as the damage I've caused. Tread lightly with those threats though." I looked over at her.

"It's not a threat!" She spat.

I chuckled. "May your next move be your best move." I turned my attention away from her because I could feel my anger rising and if they didn't get me out of here, they might've tacked on another charge.

"Oh shit, Vincent!" My mom screamed, and everyone turned in her direction as my Pop collapsed to the floor.

"Pop!" Jakari rushed over to him. The courtroom was in mayhem right now, as everyone crowded around my dad.

"What the fuck!" I yelled as I tried to move toward him, but the moment I moved, the guards were on me.

Even though they were holding me, I still tried to get to him. I needed my Pop to be alright. His life and well-being flashed across my mind, and I wasn't sure how our life would be without him in it. I knew for sure I would lose my fuckin' mind.

"Stay with us, Pop!" Jakari shouted as the tears ran down his face.

As they pulled me out of the courtroom, Trevor Sandoval was standing there with a smile on his face. One thing I could promise was that I was going to wipe that muthafucka off personally. The sounds of my mother's cries ripped through me, and I could feel the anger in me rising. Tears burned my eyes, and I tried everything in me to stop them from falling, but there was nothing I could do. Everything that was happening was so overwhelming that my tears began to fall freely down my face. I'd never been afraid of anything, but losing my Pop and hearing the pain that my mom was going through just broke me. I'm shackled up behind these walls, and there was nothing I could do to help my family right now.

Once they got me in the back, I lost it. They had me in the holding room as one of the guards grabbed a bottle of water and placed it in front of me. "I'm sorry about your father." I appreciated his gesture, and I nodded my thanks.

A few minutes later, Attorney Robinson walked into the holding room, and from the grief displayed on his face, I knew it wasn't good.

"He's breathing." He sighed. "But he's unresponsive. The paramedics are on the way, and as soon as I know something, I'll let you know. Javari, I'm sorry things didn't go the way we'd hoped for. But I promise you, I will get you out of here. I'm filing an appeal first thing in the morning." He patted me on the shoulder, and I nodded. I couldn't respond to anything right now; my world was crashing down around me. Even with all the power we thought we had, It wasn't enough to keep me out of prison and to keep my family from going through the turmoil that we're going through now. The guards placed my restraints on, and we left the room to head back to the prison. My chest was tight, and I felt like I was losing control. It was best that I stayed to myself. I knew me and any lil' thing could cause me to crash out. *Twenty fuckin' years!* I can't believe these muthafuckas hit me with a dub.

## JAVARI

***One Month Later***

I COULDN'T BELIEVE I was sitting here in this dumb-ass orange suit getting ready to be transported to my father's funeral. The day of my sentencing, he'd had a stroke, and the only thing that was keeping him alive was the machines. He was on life support for a little over two weeks when we finally decided collectively that enough was enough. He wouldn't have wanted us to keep him alive that way. My mom and brother came upstate to visit me just so that we could spend time together after his passing. We were broken, and I feel like this shit is my fault. Tori hadn't come to see me or answered any of my calls. That shit was pissing me off, and on some real shit, it hurt my damn feelings. I thought we were better than that, but I guess I was wrong. All I knew was she would have a big problem when it comes to my daughter. As much as I didn't want to bring her here, I had no choice.

There was absolutely no way that I could go twenty years and not see my child.

Today was going to be a hard fuckin' day, and I had to be strong, not just for me but for my mom and brother. I hated that I had to appear like this. However my lawyer was working on getting permission for me to at least change into a suit. I won't know if that was approved until we got there. All I knew was that I wouldn't be able to sit with my family.

"Taleo! It's time to go, sir," the guard stated as he opened my cell to put my restraints on.

C.O. Collins was transporting me; he was the same officer that gave me the water the day my Pop had the stroke. He was pretty cool, and I'd much rather he be the one to take me.

"When we get to the church, I'm going to let you have time with your family, but you have to sit with me during the services. Another guard will be with us, but he's cool, and as long as you do what we tell you, you'll be good." He strapped the restraints on my legs, and we walked out of the cell.

"I appreciate that," I told him.

"Man, you, your Pop, and your brother are legends out here in these streets. You don't know it, but you saved my life. I was living on the streets some years back, and you and your brother were coming out of this party downtown at the Ritz, and I was standing outside. I asked if you could help me get a room, and you gave me all the money in your pocket and kept walking. It was a little over a thousand dollars in that gold money clip." Hearing him tell me that story stopped me in my tracks.

"You're right. I don't remember that. But I'm glad you do and that I could help you out through a tough time. We all need a little help sometimes." I shrugged in hopes that he understood what I was saying.

Helping me out could be the start of a great business relationship. I didn't talk to many people in here, and every day a nigga was trying to offer me a service of protection. One thing about it, there wasn't shit scary in me. I'd break a nigga's neck if they ever thought about fuckin' with me.

A couple hours later, we were pulling up to my mom's church in West Philadelphia. Jakari and I were never raised in the hood, but my mother was, and she never forgot where she came from. She would always take us to the hood to see my aunts and cousins, and trust me, we enjoyed every bit of it. Linking with our cousins, Trevion and Gazi Black, is always a good time. You would've thought we all were brothers, because my mom, Chance, and my aunt Stacia were very close. Nobody, and I do mean nobody fucked with the Black brothers. They had their hands in a little bit of everything, but drugs and guns was what they were heavily involved in. My cousin, Gazi, was crazy as fuck and played no games about his family. We were a couple of hours early, and my Pop's body was already in the church, so that gave me time to see him privately.

The guards escorted me into the church then allowed me to walk up to the casket alone.

"I'm sorry, Pop," I said with regret as tears streamed down my face. "I know I let you down with the way everything went down. But I promise you, I'll lead this organization standing on the allegiance that you've always stood on. I'ma make you proud, Pop. I'll rule it with an iron fist and protect what you've built. I know that's what you would've wanted." I stood there in silence, staring at the man that had been in my life since the day I was born. My father, my hero, my leader, our foundation. I'd never let his legacy die, and I'd never stop honoring him. My heart was heavy as fuck, and all the pain that I was holding unleashed through my tears. I cried like a baby, falling to my knees. Arms wrapped around me, and I looked up and saw my teary-eyed twin brother kneeling by my side.

"I got you, bro," Jakari said, his voice cracking, and I knew this was tearing him up. Once we gathered our emotions, we stood, and Juan Hundero and my attorney, Lance Robinson, approached us.

"Javari, I've already spoken to your mother and brother when I visited the house. You know what your father meant to me. He was my best friend; I looked at Vincent as my brother. The guards here have agreed to let us have a moment in the back to handle a little bit of needed business." I turned towards the guards, and they nodded in agreement, and I saw members from our founding father's families fill into the church.

We headed to a backroom in the church that was already set up. Jakari had a suit and shoes in hand, and they allowed me to get dressed. I appreciated the guards taking the shackles off of me so that I could change freely. Jakari stepped into the dressing room, and that's when I noticed that we both were wearing the same suit, socks, and shoes. We normally would try to switch things up, just so that people could actually decipher which one of us it was which. Even my damn wife had a hard time telling us apart if we wore the same thing. The shit was crazy because I could pick her ass out in a crowded room with a blindfold on. Everything about Jakari and I were identical, so I could imagine a little confusion.

"You on your twin shit for real today, huh?" I smiled as he handed me the same pair of Cartier sunglasses that he was wearing.

"Yeah, I am. This is the best time for us to do what we need to do. We've gone over this plan several times. I know you're not a hundred percent with it, but I'm telling you, Jav, it'll work. The other Cartels know Pop has died, and you're in prison. They have been trying to step into our territories. I have hired more security, but you trying to deal with this shit behind bars doesn't work. We can switch in and out; we just have to figure out how. You and Pop have been headlining the news since your sentencing, so this shit is bound to get worse.

Tre and Gazi have stepped in to help me keep things

calm, but they got their own shit to deal with," he said to me, and I had to really think about what he was suggesting.

"In order for this to work, we need people on the inside of the prison, and I'm not sure those guards are enough to make this shit work. I don't trust anybody, Kari. You know that. If we do this, I need our people on the inside. I need for you to quickly get me everything you can get me on the warden. How will you do that shit if you're on the inside? I need your expertise on the outside, bro. You may not feel like you are, but you're a very important piece to this organization." I glanced over at him.

"I have someone that I trust with my life, and I've been working with her for a while now. She's been vetted and she'll work for us during my absence. Trust me, bro. I got us with this. Her name is Tamia, and her number is programmed in my phone. The code is our birthday. Here are my keys, wallet, and phone. You already know my information to get into my house. The test will be when we step outside those doors if the guards are able to tell the difference between us," Kari said to me.

"You sure about this, Kari?" I sighed, looking over at him.

"I'm more than sure. Attorney Robinson is working to get those charges dropped, and until then, this is what we have to do. We will work out the details once we get control of the situation," he said to me, and I stood there in my thoughts for a moment.

"Who all knows about this plan?" I asked him.

"Mace, Milan, Mom and Tamia. I had to tell Mom because she would know it's you instantly." I chuckled, hearing him say that about our mother because he was right. She birthed us, so of course she knew the difference in her children.

"I'll be running this organization as you. No one can know that we're trading places. I won't have you sitting in there long. I'm thinking a week or two and we'll move in and out like that. I have to get our team in place. But before I do that, we have to get the workers on the inside on our side. Key people like the warden, HR, and the guards that work visitation. Get me that information and I'll handle everything else." I dapped him up, giving him a hug. We put our game face on and headed out the door. The guards looked at us, and I knew then that they were confused.

"If you don't mind, can we keep those off until it's time to go? I won't do anything to jeopardize my position and y'all's job," Jakari spoke up, and I waited for them to respond.

"It's not the proper procedures, but we will allow it, sir. Damn, I must say I've never seen a set of twins look so much alike. I mean, I've seen identical twins, but there is usually something that's different about them. You guys have mastered this, right down to the visible tattoos." C.O. Collins smiled, still settling into the thought of not knowing if he's really talking to me or not. The guards tried to follow us into the room where Juan Hundero and the founding members of the INC were standing, but Juan immediately stopped them.

"Gentlemen, give us a moment. You can stand right outside of this door, and we will be out shortly." He smiled, and Collins nodded in agreement.

"Let's get down to it. Javari and Jakari, we want to again give you our deepest condolences. Javari Taleo, we're here to swear you in and know that we're working with your attorney to help you out of your situation." Juan smiled, but there wasn't a smile on my face at all.

"With all due respect, we have to get more people in our pockets. There is no way I should've been sitting this long. I know it's a situation I caused, but every member of the INC should be protected. My Pop had a way of running things, and I of course, will have a different way of operating this organization. It's time for some changes. I'll give suggestions if you don't mind taking them," I stated as I glanced around the room.

"Your input will always be welcomed." He patted me on my back, and everyone else agreed.

"Thank you." I smiled. "Let's get this done." His assistant pulled a document for me to sign, but before signing, I saw a section in the rules that I was familiar with.

### INC Rules:

*The founding fathers of the INC. Each Cartel represents your father's name and legacy. Every year in March, there is a grand meeting, and during that meeting, your Cartel leader must be present. That's where he or she will pay the Cartel yearly dues of 10% of your yearly earnings. During the meet-*

ing, the oath is recited. It's also recited if you're sworn into The INC.

I signed the document and started reciting the Oath. I didn't need to read it from anything I learned those words as a young boy, and I honored them now as a man and leader.

"I stand on the foundation of our codes. I give my loyalty and pledge to protect all things that bind us together. I will honor my brothers and stand on the shoulders of our Allegiance. No disloyalty, insubordination, or perfidy will be tolerated. I accept any consequences for those acts. Flesh of my Flesh. Blood of my Blood. I give my life for the Inc and I'll Die for the Inc." While the oath was being recited, each member cut their thumb.

Once the blood appeared, we pressed our thumbs together and that concluded my swearing in. This part was only done when someone had to be sworn in to take the reins.

"Javari, you shouldn't have any issues with the Sandavol's," Juan said as we all headed out of the room.

"I'm never worried." Is all I had to say regarding them. Jakari and I walked out the doors that lead to the outside. We wanted to walk our mom in and line up with our family. The guards were with us and decided to let me sit with my family.

"Sir, you can go ahead and sit with your family." The guard looked from me to Jakari, and I got so fuckin' amused because these niggas really couldn't tell us apart.

"Thank you." Kari was responding to their asses, and I

guess if we were going to do this, we had to make sure they believed he was me.

We walked up to the awaiting limo, and my mom's security opened the door. Then our mom stepped out of the car with my daughter Ciani and my aunt Stacia. Tori walked up to the car, and her ass was trying her best to figure out which one was me, and it was seriously sad that she couldn't tell.

"Are we talking today?" I questioned her, and she focused on me.

"Daddy!" Ciani yelled in excitement, and I gripped her up for the biggest hug.

"Hey, baby girl. I miss you so much." I kissed her face as she giggled.

"Nephew, don't look like you put up a fight with this baby. She looks just like her mama." Aunt Stacia pinched Ci's cheek, and she fell out into a fit of laughter again. She was right; my baby girl was the spitting image of her mom.

"I'm sorry, Jav. I'm just pissed right now. You know I love you and I wouldn't normally act like this. I'm sorry about your dad. You know I liked him."

"Liked! Be careful your horns are showing, Tori," Kari said to her, and I knew she was pissing him off.

I placed my daughter on her feet, and Tori grabbed her hand. It was time for us to head inside. So, Kari and I grabbed our mother's hand and led the way.

*Lord Do It for Me* by Zacardi Cortez was playing while we walked in, and it was something about that song that just

50

took over my body, and the anger in me was unbearable. I wanted my Pop alive and healthy; this shit wasn't right. The service lasted a couple of hours, and everything was just a blur. My mom put together a beautiful service for my father, he would've definitely been pleased.

"I love you. The guards are going to shackle me, and I don't want my daughter to see that. I'll call you as soon as I can." Wrapping my arms around her, I gave her a hug, and she turned to kiss my lips.

"I love you too, call me tomorrow. I'm sure I'll be with your family tonight." She kissed my lips again, stood to grab Ciani, and left out.

Once the service was over, they took Jakari to the back so that he could change into the orange suit, put the restraints on him, and got him out to the van. He looked over at me, and I nodded to let him know that I was good.

"I can't believe that you niggas are about to go in and out of prison like you niggas got some get out of jail free cards. This nigga Kari is smiling like he about to go to the strip club. Nigga, you going to prison with other niggas that ain't had pussy since pussy had the fuck them! That nigga gotta shower ass to the wall. I hope his ass comes out the way he went the fuck in, 'cause them niggas ain't all niggas they sheniggas! I'm telling you pretty muthafuckas now, don't ask me to trade places for shit. I'm allergic to prison and prison is allergic to my ass!

If I had a brother, that nigga gone have to go do his on

muthafuckin' time from the beginning! And if his ass decides to go to prison for me, you best believe I'm not swapping out with his ass later on. Fuck that! Keep yo' happy go lucky wannabe in charge and take my murder charge ass to jail or hell!" Mace went on and on. Milan was bent over, and I had to laugh at this nigga because he was stressed the fuck out.

"So, what you saying, you wouldn't have done that for me?" I asked him.

"That's exactly what the fuck I'm saying. The fuck kinda friend you thought you had! 'Cause I'm not him. I'll kill a nigga for yo' ass, sell drugs for yo' ass, rob a nigga for yo' ass, but I promise you, you gon' do that time on your damn own. I gotta give it to you; that shit y'all just pulled off was some phenomenal shit. Now let's go to the repass 'cause Aunt Stacia said she made steaks and seafood salad. None of us hood niggas want the fancy shit Mama Chance is about to serve." Mace walked off towards his car.

"We'll talk at your mom's house." Milan gave me a hug and walked off behind Mace.

I walked towards Jakari's car, and I just sat here taking all of this in. I couldn't believe I was out, and the shit that Jakari talked me into actually worked. Well, I wouldn't know that it worked until he got back inside and called me. I do know this, shit with the Taleo Cartel was about to change. Any mutha-fucka that even thought about coming for us or moving in on any of our territories would die. I wanted to let my wife in on what was happening, but something was telling me to hold off on that so that's exactly what I did.

# JAKARI

I HAD to figure out something to get my brother out of the situation I caused. I wasn't a troublemaker, but one thing I didn't deal with was disrespect. We had run-ins with the Sandoval's several times, but nothing to the extent that had us ready for war. Ziek knew what to say and what not to say when it came to us. I guess he felt like he wanted to show he was that nigga and start some shit with the Taleo's at the Monster's Ball. He fucked around and found out that that was the wrong move to make. What's fucking with me is all of this shit was over a bitch.

I know he sent her to fuck with me. I guess he assumed I was the weakest link. I was that nigga that would always give you those fuck around and find out moments. I will pull your cap back for fucking with me or my family. The night in the club turned bad, and I tried to walk away, but it was the moment the nigga spit in my face and pulled his gun on me that caused me to black out and put that bullet between his eyes.

I would never openly cause embarrassment to my family, and I haven't said anything to my mom or brother, but it was all my fault that my brother was in jail and that our Pop died. He had that stroke because he fought hard as hell to get Javari out of there. We had so many conversations, and he'd even yelled at me and in so many words, called me a disgrace to the family. He didn't say that word exactly, but he might as well have said it. It wasn't a good conversation, even after he knew the context that brought me to my boiling point. I'd always known that Javari was the son he loved the most. He showed it, but Jav always told me that I was overthinking it. That Pop loved us the same, but what he didn't know was that I knew for a fact he didn't love us the same because I overheard him explaining that shit to my mom.

Yes, I loved my Pop, and losing him hurt all of us. But on some real shit, he wasn't good enough for my mom. That dude had been cheating on her for years and had a daughter with his side bitch who would be graduating college this year. I knew all of this because I'd traveled with him, and I set up his security detail. Not to mention when some shit just doesn't seem right, you investigate. I'm a genius when it comes to this technology shit, so hiding anything from me is laughable.

I'ma find out everything on yo' ass, right down to what the fuck you had for dinner the night before, no matter if you cooked that shit or ordered it from your favorite restaurant. I'm my mother's son, and I'd do whatever I had to do to protect her and that includes protecting her from my Pop. I went to her about it after she had just found out about him cheating on her. They still were not on the best of terms when he died because she'd just found out about his infidelity a few months before his passing, and so did I.

I wish I would've found out sooner, but it wasn't until recently that I started to get suspicious. Dude had been doing shit with this woman for so long that he had a whole damn kid out here. Javari and I have a baby sister, and I'm not even sure how to even process that. Javari doesn't know any of this. I planned to tell him, but I knew that it would taint his memories of our dad. Loyalty to him is big, as it is to me, and if he found out that my Pop wasn't loyal to our mom, there isn't no telling what his ass would do. I just had to find the right time to tell him, because at some point, we were going to have to go meet our sister.

I couldn't believe that I was sitting here in a prison cell and that the shit we just pulled worked. I'd been here for two days, and this shit was crazy as fuck. I hoped and prayed that we found a way out of this shit because a nigga needed my Purple mattress. This hard ass thin mattress ain't it. I was ready to go call my brother and tell his ass to donate Purple brand fuckin' mattresses and pillows to all the inmates in this muthafucka just so I could get me one. Prison ain't for me!

"Dinner!" The C.O. called out and our cell doors started making that clinking sound as they opened.

I let out a sigh because I'd much rather sit in this mutha-

56

fucka and starve, but I knew I needed to go eat just to keep my energy up. You just never know what was going to go down in here. These niggas were shiesty as fuck, and because I was a Taleo, I didn't know if they were trying to get next to me to create an allegiance or to take my ass out. Walking out of the cell, a breath got caught in my throat. I for sure stopped breathing for a second. I'd been around beautiful women all my life and damn sure had my share of them but never has a woman caused my life to flash before my eyes. I'm exaggerating of course, but I stopped breathing for a milla second.

Ms. Beautiful stood there with an unreadable expression. She didn't seem like she belonged in this environment. For the last couple of days, I'd been studying these C.O.'s and the women officers seemed hard, like they could take these niggas if they had to do so. She seemed different though; all I saw besides her beauty was nervousness. I didn't think this job was for her.

"Damn, you fine!" One of the inmates yelled out, and I felt myself getting pissed like shorty belonged to me. I had to shake that shit off, but he was right she was indeed fine as fuck.

The beauty this woman possessed had me zoned out. Her deep brown skin was smooth and blemish-free, and her mesmerizing brown eyes, pointy nose, and pouty lips only enhanced her beauty. I stood there gazing at her like I was some simp ass nigga. I had to force myself to move as my chest felt like it was tightening up, and I prayed your boy wasn't having a heart attack. This feeling was something I'd never felt before, and I damn sure didn't want to feel that shit right now. Now wasn't the time to get caught the fuck up. Maybe my ass had been locked up too long—fuck that, two days was still too long.

I made a mental note to tell Jav he needed to hurry and get things in place because I needed to get out of here. Once her eyes locked with mine, a slight smile flashed across her face, and all of a sudden, going to dinner wasn't a bad idea.

When I approached her, I decided to speak. "Sup," I spoke, and just as she was about to speak back, this other hatin' ass C.O. stepped up.

"Keep it moving," he yelled. I looked at this dude and was about to address his ass when I thought about it. I didn't need to create beef when it wasn't any. So, I kept it moving and headed into the cafeteria. I grabbed a tray, and my expression instantly turned into a frown when I saw that they were serving niggas. Grabbing an apple and orange, I decided to just eat that. There was no way I was eating that slop they called dinner. I think it was sloppy joes, but that shit looks ashy as fuck. About an hour later, I was back in my cell waiting on my time to use the phone.

Thank God Javari had a MP3 player, and I guess they sold the shit here so that we could listen to music. I laid back on the bed and decided to chill out. I was surprised to see Ms. Beautiful walk up to my cell.

"I saw that you didn't eat, and I know you must be

hungry. I was able to sneak this back here. It's not much, just some chicken and shrimp alfredo that I made. I promise you it's safe. I just felt bad because I saw that you didn't eat. Here is a soda to drink as well." She handed me the food and drink, and I had to smile because that was thoughtful of her. Then it hit me: if she was giving me her food, what was she going to eat?

"Thank you for thinking of me. But what are you going to eat if you're offering me your dinner?" I leaned against the cell door, waiting for her response.

"We had a birthday party for one of the C.O.'s, and I forgot about it. We had food, so I ate that." She smiled.

"What's your name?" I asked her.

"Nia. What's yours?"

"Something tells me you already know my name. It's nice to meet you though, Nia." I smiled and took the food from her hands. "I really do appreciate this. I'ma pray it up to God that you're not trying to kill me. If you are trying to kill me, I'ma make sure I kill yo' ass again when you make it to the other side," I chuckled.

"What! If you're dead, how the hell would I die in the first place?" she asked with a confused expression.

"Watch who you befriend and share your dinner with, lovely." I winked, and I was sure baby girl was going to do her homework and find out who Javari was. I almost fucked up and gave her my name. For now, she had to think that she was messing with Jav. And damn, that shit sucked!

59

JAVARI

**Two Weeks Later**

I'D BEEN STAYING at my brother's crib because of course I had to act as him. It'd only been a couple of weeks, and it was hard as fuck not to go over to my crib and fall deep into the sweetness of my wife's walls. I missed the shit out of that girl, and I damn sure missed my daughter. Even though Tori had been acting funny towards me, I understood her anger. So, I decided that I would go over there tonight and tell her everything. I trusted my wife, so I knew that she wouldn't repeat none of what I was about to tell her. The doorbell sounded, and it was Tamia, the chick that Kari said would be helping us. I'd actually been working with her ever since the day we made the switch. I was about to go back in, and I needed to know that we had everything in place so that I could use it when I got back on the inside. I opened the door then stepped aside so that she could enter.

"Hey. I got some good stuff," she said as she took a seat and pulled out her laptop."Starting with the warden, he's cheating on his wife and has been for the last three years. The interesting part about this is he's cheating on her with another man. His name is Dondre Jones and he's an inmate at the prison you're in. His location is on cell block D. Janice Sullivan, is the head of HR at the prison, and she doesn't have anything going on other than she knows what the warden is up to and covers it up. In return, she does what she wants to do around there.

Lt. Michaels is the executive director over the C.O.'s, who beat an inmate to a bloody pulp, and they pushed it under the rug. Of course, I have the footage. These are the key players in the prison, and with this information, I think we got them. I used the list of names that work for the Taleo Cartel and took the liberty of applying for jobs. Once they get inside, I'm sure Janice can help get them into the positions that we need them in."

"Damn! This is good shit. Were you able to get anything on the list of judges I sent you?" I looked over at her.

"Yes, I did." She grabbed her messenger bag and pulled out a thick file. "This is a lot, but everything in this file should get you exactly what you need. Hopefully, your lawyer can use this information and get you exonerated," she stated as she packed up her things to leave.

"Man, I appreciate this. I gotta let Kari know that you

need to stay on the team. I'm not gonna lie; I was skeptical at first, but you proved me wrong." I smiled because shorty really ended up coming through for a nigga. Big time.

We spoke for a few more minutes before she left. Then I walked over to the bar to make myself a drink. For the first time in a long time, I felt good. I was in control of the Taleo Cartel and had an upcoming meeting with Draius Chandler. My Pop and I had been trying to get a meeting with the Chandler's for a few years. The Chandler Cartel was one of the biggest, if not the largest Cartel in the world. Pop has always said if we could just join forces with the Chandler's that our family would be set for life. So many had tried to bridge the gap with them, but it never worked out. Draius Chandler didn't trust a damn soul. This partnership would open up more ports for us to ship out of. It would be a lucrative deal for everyone involved.

My phone beeped with a text from Milan, jolting me out of my thoughts. I pulled up the message as a sharp pain shot through my heart, and that alone caused my anger to rise. I was ready to spit fuckin' fire, and nobody was safe. Pulling out my personal phone that I used for Tori, I clicked on her name and called her.. The line rang a few times then went to voicemail, indicating that she had forwarded my call. I immediately dialed her ass again with pure fury flowing through my veins.

"Hello," she answered on the first ring.

"Sup, baby girl. What you up to?" I asked, just to see what she'd say.

"Nothing much. I'm home in bed, thinking about you." I could hear a muffled noise in the background, but there. My gut told me she was lying.

"Why does it sound like you're in a club?" I questioned, already grabbing my keys and making my way out the door.

"Nah, that's just the television, babe. Steph is calling; she's been arguing with Shaun. Let me call you right back. Stay by your phone." She rushed to end the call before I could say anything else. I immediately dialed Milan.

"Hey, bro. I sent his picture to Tamia, she said she'll get me what I need on him soon. You need me to handle anything right now?" she asked.

"Nah, I got it from here." I ended the call and headed toward the house I shared with my wife.

When I pulled up, I instantly set eyes on Tori's car that was parked right out front. It was late, so I figured Ciani was with my mom since her ass was out and probably just getting home. I stepped inside, and the house was quiet. She wasn't in our bedroom, but I heard the shower running, so I trekked upstairs smoothly, easing into the bathroom. A pregnancy test on the counter caught my attention, and my jaw clenched as my damn stomach felt like it was twisted into a knot.

*I'ma kill this bitch!*

My beeping phone alerted her that I was standing there watching her causing her to nearly jump out of her own skin.

"Jakari, what the fuck! Why the fuck are you in my shit? Get out!" she screamed.

I stared at her for the longest while she was still cursing, thinking that I was my brother.

"All these years that we've been married, and you still don't know who I am when I'm in front of your face?" I grimaced.

"You're identical. How am I supposed to figure it out, Jav!" she said to me with a confused look on her face.

"My voice, the love that we share, the way I look at you, that's how you're supposed to know."

"Wait— how—how did you get out!" As if it finally registered that it was me standing here in the flesh, she ran over to me, planting kisses on my lips, but I pushed her back lightly. Through her excitement to see me, she'd forgotten her little pregnancy test. But I was damn sure going to remind her about that shit.

"So, tell me. Are we expecting a new addition to the family?" I questioned, as my phone beeped again and the nervousness in her eyes appeared while her body started to tremble. I glanced down at my phone, and it was a text from Tamia.

Tamia: The man in the picture with your wife is a local plug, TI Martin. He receives distribution from the Taleo distro center East. He's been in the shipment log for a few years now. But he's known your wife for about eight years. It seems that they used to date from high school up until sophomore year in college.

Sliding my phone back into my pocket, I turned my attention back to my now-crying wife.

"Javari, please!" she pleaded, but I wasn't trying to hear shit she had to say.

I snatched the pregnancy test off the counter just as she attempted to lunge for it. However, there was no stopping me from reading the results. Seeing the pink pregnant sign in the middle caused my anger to erupt like a fuckin' active Volcano. I lost all sense of religion on her hoe ass!

"Why all the tears, Tori? What, I know yo' dumb ass ain't think a nigga was gon' just believe this was my baby. Yo' sneaky pussy ass couldn't have been that fucking delusional!" I growled, roughly tapping her forehead.

*Whap!*

"*You* did this shit to us! I wouldn't have to fuck the next nigga if you were home to fuck me!" She spat as I stood still in disbelief that she'd slapped the fuck outta me.

My stomach tightened, and my hands clenched by my side. I was fighting with everything in me to not lose it, but that shit went out the window because who the fuck did she think that she was dealing with? Never had I ever had to treat my wife like this, but this bitch had me all types of fucked up. Gripping her by the neck, I drove her head into the toilet that was still filled with the piss she'd just done her test with.

"Don't you *ever* put your fuckin' hands on me, bitch!" My trigger finger twitched. My blood boiled. My vision blurred with rage. I had given this woman every fuckin' thing— a beautiful home, unconditional love, loyalty. And she had the audacity to betray me! I took a deep breath as I heard her gasping for air and gargling piss bubbles, and I knew if I kept going, I would've drowned her. This was damn sure the end of us, though. I couldn't deal with someone that wasn't loyal to me or faithful to our marriage. I was done. Finally, releasing her, I stepped back and watched as she yanked her head back and gasped for air.

"Pack your shit and get the fuck out of my house! Leave everything that came with this marriage the fuck here! You don't get to live off my shit with the next nigga. You're married to a fuckin' BOSS, and yo' loose pussy ass is out here fuckin' the help! I can't believe this shit. You really thought since I was in jail that you and your nigga was gon' eat off the muthafuckin' table that I built! Bitch! I will knock all this shit over with you and your bitch nigga in it.

I'll fuckin' put a toe tag on you and that nigga, don't ever fuckin' play with me! I'ma teach you a lesson though. You better hope that nigga can take care of you cause you not walking away from here with shit but the clothes on your back. No money, no credit cards, no cars, no jewelry, none of the expensive ass clothes or shoes I bought you. Nothing! Go see what your new nigga can do for you!" I roared, roughly shoving her naked body to the bathroom door.

"Yo' ass don't even have the decency to cover your shit up. You know my people are out here. You foul as fuck. I really thought you were my lifelong partner when you were nothing but a simp ass bitch!" she stood there in tears with her hair drenched, and her lips trembling like she was the fuckin' victim.

"Get the fuck outta my shit! And don't think for one second that my daughter is going with you!" My voice bounced off the bathroom walls.

I had to get the fuck out of here now. I glared at her once more then turned to walk out of the bathroom. She must have thought about all that I'd said and realized her lifestyle, as she knew it was over because she took off behind me and followed me out to the garage. Ass naked.

"Jav, please don't do this! I'm so sorry, baby. I'll get rid of it and make things right with you. I can't lose you," she cried, but I kept it moving.

I ignored her, deciding not to drive Jakari's car. Instead, I got on my motorcycle and cranked it up. The engine roared, drowning out whatever she was saying. Without a thought, I hit the button to let the garage door up and peeled out of the driveway, gripping the handles tightly.

The second I hit the highway, my rage simmered, but not all the way. Trust me, I could paint the city red and send the crime rate up in a matter of hours. Truthfully, Tori's whore ass wasn't even worth it, and that was the only reason why I didn't. Since I was still riding, I told Siri to call Mace and listened to my air pods ring.

"Yeah," he answered immediately.

"Meet me at the warehouse," I stated.

"Nigga, did you catch a body at the warehouse, 'cause ain't shit there but drugs, the shooting range, funeral home, and money? And I know damn well you don't think I'm getting my ass out there in that damn field to pick no weed. Y'all better hope the leader of free world that just got elected don't come for y'all asses. You know this nigga just called the Mexican Cartel terrorists! I wonder what the fuck he gon' call you niggas that's sitting here right under his nose. Bruh, when he finds out that his good ole U.S. of fuckin A got just as many Cartel's in it, his ass gon' blow his toupee. You niggas gon' be under the jail. But here I come." This crazy nigga is something special because I was still trying to figure out how the fuck we got on all of this when all I asked him to do was meet me at the warehouse.

It took me an hour to get there, but the ride was necessary. By the time I pulled up, my head was clearer, even though I was still ready to murder a nigga. I punched in the code, disarmed the system, and stepped inside. Something was definitely off, so I pulled my gun out. The light in my apartment above the gun range was on. My brows creased because nobody was supposed to be there. I rearmed the system then made my way up the stairs with my senses on high alert. I heard soft singing coming from inside.

"Happy birthday to me, happy birthday to me..."

*The fuck is going on!*

Easing the door open, my hand gripped my gun tightly. I was taken aback because, damn, this woman was fuckin' beautiful. Her fine ass stood in my space, wearing my tank top and a pair of briefs that had no chance against all that ass. Thick thighs, smooth skin, curves for days. Who the hell was she? Her ass seemed too damn comfortable up in here. Was she a squatter? Did her ass just take it upon herself to move into my shit? But how? This place was in the middle of nowhere. I had so many damn questions, but I was so stuck that I couldn't even form the words that I needed to say. Then, I noticed the wine glass in her hand. My expensive ass wine at that, and that revived my ass, causing the frown on my face deepen.

"Who the fuck are you? And where is Jakari?" She turned to face me, locking eyes with me, and I saw confusion in her gaze.

"He never said anything about having a twin. Oh hell, I guess he wouldn't tell me anything like that, considering they kidnapped me. I must say y'all are the nicest set of kidnappers I've met, being as though you dummies kidnapped me from someone that had already kidnapped me." She shrugged, and I stiffened.

"Kidnapped!" I repeated. "The fuck is you talking about? My family isn't into no shit like that."

She must've been mistaken. She folded her arms and rested to one side with her hip extended, and that move had a nigga feeling warm. I'd never in my life reacted like this to a woman that I just laid eyes on.

"Shorty, I'm sure there must be some kind of mistake. We don't do shit like this. What's your name, and how long have you been here?"

"I'm Jade, and I've been here for a little over three months. The dark-skinned chick, Milan, kidnapped me. She said she was ordered to do so but that I wouldn't get hurt. They just needed to send a message to my boyfriend. I didn't say anything to correct her because I was pissed and scared that this kept happening to me. But when Jakari started to come around, we became friends, and he promised he wouldn't let anyone hurt me. I haven't seen Milan since the day she left me here though. Jakari's been coming by to restock the fridge so that I can cook, and he brings me the personal things I need. Oh, and if you're the one handling that now, my list is over there." She pointed toward the counter like she was running shit.

I blinked; my anger was pushed out of the way by my amusement. Because I know damn well this chick didn't think I was going to the store to get things off of a grocery list.

I'ma a boss in real life, so this ain't it. I glanced at the counter, then back at her.

"So, let me get this straight. You're saying my family kidnapped you? But yet you're in here sipping on my expensive bottle of Chateau Latour, cooking, and making a grocery list. It even looks like you have an iPad over there, so I'll assume you have wifi. It doesn't look like you've been kidnapped to me."

She chuckled. **"**So, you expected me to be tied to a chair and brutally beaten before you believed that I was kidnapped? Clearly, they didn't want me dead. I don't have wifi. I love to cook so Jakari filled this tablet up with hundreds of recipes so that I could try them out." I heard what she was saying, but I had to get down to the bottom of this shit.

"Well, since you're here, you might as well stay for dinner. It would be nice to have some company for my birthday. Oh, and what's your name?" she turned to give her attention to whatever it was she was cooking. It smelt good as shit, as my stomach growled.

It was crazy because I was really standing here contemplating having dinner with her. Even though she's saying we kidnapped her, it was something about her that brought calmness to me in that moment. That had never happened before.

"I'm Javari," I finally replied, stepping closer to the kitchen.

"Cute." She offered a light smile. "Dinner will be ready

in ten minutes. Help yourself to some wine." She turned and burst into a cute lil' laugh.

*The fuck is going on with me! What the fuck is cute? I'm a gangsta; cute is only in my vocabulary when I'm speaking to my daughter.*

"I'll be right back," I said to her as I turned and headed back downstairs to the first level of the warehouse. I immediately dialed Milan's number.

"Hey, what's up?" she spoke when she answered the call.

"Yo, who the fuck is the chick in my apartment?" I questioned.

"Ohhhh shit! I forgot about that bitch. I swear I did. Your dad was having a fallout with Javier Forelli, and Forelli ran his drugs through one of our ports without approval. Not only that, but he threatened to kill all of you if your dad didn't back off. So, he sent me to send a message loud and clear. Your dad wanted me to take something that meant a lot to Forelli. I saw him out on his grounds several times, having lunch with his girl. So, I figured I would just snatch her ass up. Your Pop thought that would get him in line, but it didn't—the nigga got worse.

This all took place while you were locked up. I think folk knew you were your dad's muscle, and when you got locked up, shit got a lil' choppy. He never said anything else about her, never gave any other orders on her, and I truly just forgot her ass was there. Look at it this way, you just found out that your bitch of a wife ain't shit. Treat it as some welcome home pussy; payback is the best get-back. Nigga, it's been a minute since you had some, so this works out. You welcome!" she laughed and ended the call.

"Yizzzo!" I heard Mace yell out, walking into the warehouse.

"Sup. I need you to cut distro on this nigga. I just sent you his information.

"Nigga, I know you lyin! Why the hell couldn't you tell me that shit over the phone? I was watching CNN, smoking on some of that backyard Ganja y'all growing out back and drinking me some damn liquor! I drove all the fuckin' way out here thinking we had to body a nigga or two-" He stopped speaking and looked past me, so I turned to see what he was looking at.

Jade was standing at the top of the stairs. "Javari, dinner is ready," she called out.

"Who in the fine fuck is that? Nigga, you out here cheating on Tori!" He looked from me to Jade. "I'm proud as fuck of you 'cause that chick is money hungry as fuck. She's not right for you; I was just waiting for you to see it." He smiled, patting me on the back. I looked at this nigga like he was crazy.

"So, you didn't know that she was here?" I looked over at him.

"Know she was here? Hell nawl, why would I know that? Who is she?" He shot questions back-to-back.

"Lan kidnapped her. She got orders from my Pop to do it." I shrugged.

"Kidnapped! Hell to the nawl! How long her ass been an abductee? Nigga, you think you got twenty years now. They gon' put y'all asses under the jail and I can promise you I ain't going with you. Don't call my ass back out here until her fine ass is gone!" He sighed, shaking his head and pulling his flask out to take a drink. This nigga was throwed, I swear.

"Bruh, you really need to stop drinking and smoking. That shit is fucking with your mental." I shook my head at him. "Just make sure you handle that shit with this nigga. Tori's been cheating on me with his bitch ass. Ain't nan muthafucka gon' eat from my table, fuck my wife, and live to talk about it." Cutting off his supply was just the beginning of the bullshit I was about to do to this nigga.

"Nigga, just gon' and kill his ass. Why y'all always gotta prolong the shit! A bullet to the head is just as effective. But whatever yo' murderous ass wants to do, I guess I'm in. I'm just not with this kidnapping shit though, and her lil fine ass coming out here talking 'bout '*Javari, dinner's ready.*' Bitch! This nigga is a stone-cold murderer; his daddy had you kidnapped! The fuck kind of kidnapping is this any damn way?

My suggestion is to let shorty go and hang up the kidnapping business 'cause you niggas clearly need a class on that shit. Kidnapping 101: How the fuck is she in there wit' a hot stove cooking you dinner? Nigga, she gon' poison yo' ass or burn you alive! You betta not eat shit from her, fuck around, and your tongue gon' be hanging out the side of your mutha-fuckin' neck. Nigga, please don't let pussy be the reason somebody takes you the fuck out. Let me get my ass out of here and back to being unbothered. When I'm around you niggas, I become bothered as fuck." He turned to leave while I was shaking my damn head.

I couldn't help but laugh at my best friend because no matter how gangsta we were, he would bust his guns and let you know he wasn't fucking with you at the same time. Just as I was about to head back up to speak with Jade, my phone started ringing. I saw that it was Jakari calling, so I quickly answered.

"Sup, bro," I spoke as soon as I accepted the call.

"Man, I'm losing weight in this bitch. But everything is good. I spoke to Tamia, and she told me y'all were setting everything up."

"Yeah, man. I'll be making the switch with you in about a week. But yo' did you forget to tell me we had a visitor in my apartment?" I questioned.

"Ohhh shit, Jade! Yeah, man. That was something Pop did. But don't hurt her, she's a good person. When he died, things just kind of went left, and I forgot about her. She's cool, just in a bad position right now. Let her go, but something is going on with her situation. I was trying to dig deeper into it, but then Pop got sick, and I let it go. See what you can find out from her; she really doesn't talk about her family. All I know is who Pop snatched her from isn't her real family and they snatched her ass too. I feel bad about that. I really want to help her though. She doesn't deserve this," he expressed.

I still had to do my homework on Ms. Jade, but hurting her wasn't something I was planning to do. I'd just met her, so I'd be playing this situation close. I talked to Kari for a few more minutes before ending the call and heading back inside. It was the craziest thing—not once since I'd been here had I thought about my situation with my wife, and I got this sense of calmness around her. I knew I just met her, and I knew this kidnapping shit wasn't what went on beneath the surface. I wasn't sure what the fuck my Pop had going on, but this wasn't it.

JADE

I COULDN'T BELIEVE there was two of them, but it was something about this one that intrigued me. I could tell that he knew nothing about my kidnapping, and when I learned that they really weren't out to hurt me, that gave me such a relief. I hadn't told them much, except that I was previously kidnapped by the people they took me from. I wasn't actually sure why I was kidnapped, but something told me that it had everything to do with my cousins, who worked closely with my dad. They wanted so badly to take his spot when he passes away, but I was the only child, and my dad had let it be known that everything he owned would be given to his only daughter. That's when I would decide what I wanted to do with the family business. My father had been battling lung cancer for years now.

About a year ago, the doctors told us that he didn't have much longer to live. The Chandler Cartel was the largest Cartel in the world, and to be honest, I was a girl's girl. So, naturally, I didn't want anything to do with the business. It's my birthday and I'm celebrating it with my kidnappers. What kind of shit is that? This wasn't the life I wanted to live, not to mention the real reason why I was kidnapped the first time. So, no. I wanted nothing to do with this shit. If something happened to my dad, I was selling this shit to the highest bidder.

"Happiest of birthdays to you, Jade. If you don't mind me asking, how old are you?" Javari asked as he forked his pasta.

"Now you know you're not supposed to ask a woman her age." I smiled, pouring some more wine into my glass. "I'm thirty."

"Really? I just turned thirty-two last month." He leaned back in his seat.

Damn, this man was beautiful. His entire being screamed powerful, demanding, intense, yet loving and sexy as hell. I glanced down at his hand, and for the first time, I noticed his wedding ring, and my little feelings were crushed. I know it sounded crazy, but have you ever met someone and being in that person's space instantly moved you? That's what the hell was going on with me; he intrigued the hell out of me.

"Oh yeah, I keep forgetting you and Jakari are twins. I made him some cupcakes for his birthday. Did he at least share them with you?" I questioned, looking over at him.

"Nah, I wasn't around. I'm sure he enjoyed them, though. It seems that you and my brother were cool," he stated while shifting in his seat.

"He's just nice to me, and I really appreciated it. Even

though I was kidnapped, he tried his best for it not to seem that way. I've been through a lot lately. I've been away from home for almost a year, and I'm not sure who I can trust right now. I guess somebody really wants me to suffer." I shrugged.

"What family are you connected to? I'm only asking you that because I'm trying to figure out why the Forelli's felt the need to grip you up?"

"If you don't mind, I'd rather not say right now. I can't tell you the real reason why, because I don't know. But I know that it has something to do with my family. I need to figure things out before I bring anyone else into this. Not to mention my situation here." I sipped on my wine.

"Understood. We'll work through whatever this is and figure out our next move. I normally come here when I need to calm down and blow off some steam. Since my space is being utilized, I'ma go ahead and get out of here. But before I leave, I'll be downstairs in my gun range for a few," he said to me.

"Ok. Jakari has gone down to use it a few times. I know that I might be in the way, but it's two bedrooms here, feel free to stay. I promise I won't bother you. I'm in the smaller bedroom, so the master bedroom is available," I told him, and he nodded.

I wasn't sure if he would stay, but he could if he wanted to. After all, it was his apartment anyway. I cleared the dishes but wanted to still be around my new friend, so I headed down to the gun range to join him. When I walked in, he was reloading his gun. I placed some earplugs in my ear and eased beside him, placing my hand on his gun.

Surprisingly, he let me have it. I guess he wasn't worried about me turning his gun on him. I quickly aimed the gun, focusing on my target, and smoothly emptied the clip. He was standing there looking at me like I was crazy. I guess he wasn't expecting that out of me.

"Damn, lil mama. The clip, though, and it was all head shots." He smiled as he took the gun out of my hand and started reloading it.

"Yeah, my dad had me trained because he said we lived in crazy times, and I needed to know how to protect myself. I wanted to come down and hang out with you a little more. Thank you for being kind to me. You're a little uptight, but you did good. Anyway, I just wanted to thank you. I'm going to turn it in for the night. Hope to see you at breakfast." I walked off, but I could feel him watching me. That made me smile.

"Good morning." I smiled as Javari walked out of his bedroom. "I see you decided to stay out here."

"Yeah, it was needed." He returned my smile, pulling a seat up at the table. I sat the plate of scrambled eggs, turkey bacon, and toast in front of him.

"Can I ask you a question?" This question had been fucking with me all night.

"Let's see if I have an answer for you." I smiled, turning to face him..

"How did you know instantly that I wasn't Jakari? We're identical twins."

"Your nose is a little sleeker than his, your facial expression is a little more tense, and your eyes are just a shade darker than Jakari's. Oh, and your cheekbones is a tad bit higher than your brothers. Yes, you're identical, and I'm sure a lot of people would never look at those things. But I don't know, I'm a little different when it comes to things like that." I shrugged, and he just sat there in silence staring at me.

"I've never heard anyone do that. I'm impressed; the only person that can tell us apart is our mother."

"And now me," I laughed. "I'll be outside if you need me," I told him, grabbing my basket and heading out back.

About twenty minutes later, he came outside, and from the way he was looking, I knew that he was going to say something about me planting my vegetables near their weed pasture. Yes, they had acres and acres of weed out here. I planned to grab myself some before I went back in. This shit was the best weed I'd ever had. I be out here in the middle of nowhere, high as a Georgia pine. Just as I got my planting hole the way I wanted it, Javari was walking over to me.

"What are you doing, Shorty?" He asked me.

"I'm planting some cabbage, squash, tomatoes, and cucumbers. Oh, and my favorite fruit, strawberries and Mangos. I asked Jakari to pick these up in my last order. I'm just getting around to planting them. I hope you don't mind. I know it's close to your weed, but I promise it won't hurt anything," I told him.

"Actually, it may not hurt my plants, but you're planting your garden in its soil. Hell, it might do something to your garden. How about you plant them over there by the storage. This is one of my biggest weed supply chains out here. They will be out here to pick all of this soon, and I'd hate for them to mess up your garden," he said to me, and I frowned.

I frowned because they were about to take the damn weed. I needed to go and get me some before they took it. I wondered if I asked, would he be upset? I headed inside, but I would damn sure be back out later on. Javari was on the phone downstairs, so I decided to look through the recipes that Jakari had put on my iPad to see what I wanted to try for dinner. Javari came inside and he stood at the door watching me. That made me a little nervous, and I was just about to ask him what was wrong, but he started speaking.

"Jade, I'm not sure what your folk got you into. But I don't want to hold you here. I just spoke to my brother, and we both agree that you don't deserve this. You're free to leave, and if you tell me where to take you, I'll make sure you get there safely."

"Who's leaving?" I frowned. "Nah, I'm good right here. You can leave, but I'ma keep my kidnapped ass right here. I'd appreciate some cable and internet since I'm a free girl. Oh, and maybe a lil' car so that I can go do my own shopping. Other than that, I'm good right here," I said, placing a piece of the cut-up mango in my mouth.

I know he was confused as fuck because he looked like it. I know I should've been running for the door, especially when the people that kidnapped you said you could leave. But nah, I was good right here, tucked away from the world. I wasn't leaving until I figured out what happened and why it happened to me. Maybe my newfound friends could help me after all.

## JAKARI

Two weeks had passed, and Javari still hadn't switched out with me. He had a few more loose ends to tie up to make sure we had things together here on the inside. My brother deserved to be in that position because he was a mastermind when it came to this shit. He moved with intention, and his moves were deliberate and calculated. He was always trying to get our Pop to push the needle so that we could elevate our organization, and his views never aligned with our father's vision. This meant that there was always that constant tug of power.

Javari would never go against our Pop, and he was damn sure never going to disrespect him. He looked up to our Pop, and until I found out about the disrespectful manner in which he treated our mom, I did too. I decided to hold off on telling Javari what I'd found out because he was in prison and up against the hardest challenge we'd ever been tested with. At first, I was ready to get out of here for a little while, but then I thought about the bigger plan in all of this. We had to see this through, and I knew that Jav was out there doing his thing because shit in here was starting to shift to our advantage. Today, a few of our security guards were now guards at the prison on this block. I should've known Nick would be in here. He was head of Javari's security detail, and who better to protect him in here? Just as I stood from my bunk to take a piss, Nick walked up to the cell.

"Javari's on the visitation list, but he has that meeting with the Chandlers in a couple of weeks. He sent you this to keep you occupied." He passed me the large manilla envelope, and inside was my laptop. I could've cried seeing my damn computer. That shit had me happy as hell. I was able to do my job and be involved in what was going on, on the outside.

"I'm good. He needs to rock out and get everything we need done in place. I have the burner; you are here with me, and I have my computer, so I'm good." I shrugged.

"Yeah, I actually won't be back until Javari gets back in here. He needs me out there with him. Timothy, and Ron are both in here, and Jamarri is set to get processed in a few days. If you need anything, just let one of them know, and they will get the message to the warden. He is fully in our back pocket, and that means we have the run of this prison. Until your brother has been released from prison, at least thirty of our men will be working here. They'll be checking in visitors, working in the cafeteria to make sure that you both are having foods worth eating, so that means everyone will be eating well

in here. Javari is working that out now, and it should be imple-
mented in about a week," he said to me.

"That's good to know because this food is shit in here."
We spoke for a few more minutes before he had to leave.

I was happy about the extra time, that meant I got to
spend a little more time with Nia. She was indeed leaving her
mark on me, and I was interested in getting to know her
better. I wasn't ready for the relationship shit, but I also
wasn't against seeing what was up with her. I mean, she was
in a relationship, and if shit got deeper, shorty was going to
have to get rid of her dude. That was the only way this shit
with me was going to work. I wasn't interested in being the
face of our organization, but please believe that I would bust
my shit on a nigga quicker than my brother would. I stayed in
the background minding my tech life business but would
show the fuck up and out before a nigga could think or blink.

Nia didn't work every day, but when she did, she always
made sure to work on my block. She made sure she brought
me food, some of my favorite books, and crossword puzzles. I
spoke to Tamia and got her to meet up with her so that she
could bring me a burner phone. Once she got it, she figured
out how to sneak it in, and I was happy as hell because I
needed that damn phone. I appreciated everything Nia had
done for me. Having her be there for me these past couple of
weeks had kept me occupied. I'd learned so much about her
through conversation. She was twenty-eight and had recently
graduated with a business degree. She said after graduation,

job placement was scarce and that her friend helped her get this job.

Even though I knew so much about her, she didn't know a damn thing about me. Shit, she thought I was my brother. I wasn't sure why she was risking it all instantly to help me. I mean, the shit with us just clicked immediately, and a few days later, she was ready to smuggle in a phone for me. Even though I was going to take the phone, it caused a red flag. I took a step back to watch her moves and study her. I even had Tamia pull everything on her that she could find, and what she couldn't find, I would. Now that I had my computer, I could finally read what she had sent me. I was stretched out on my bunk when I heard her voice.

"Hey, how's your day going?" I looked up to see Nia standing outside my cell with a smile on her face.

"I'm good, beautiful. How was your day off?" I asked, sitting up.

"It was good, but I missed talking to my friend." She leaned up against the cell door.

"I'm not sure if I'm buying what you're selling, lil mama. I tried to call you last night, but I guess you were busy." I shrugged, watching her closely. I guess me staring at her was fucking with her because she dropped her head and looked away.

"Yeah, I was a little busy yesterday. I'm sorry," she stated as she turned and looked away. I wasn't sure what that was about, but we had to fix that shit.

"If you want me to believe you, you gotta stand on what you say. You can't even look at me when you're talking to me. I'm sure it's true that you missed talking to me, but you did nothing to change that. You gotta move differently when dealing with me. I'm allergic to bullshit and don't deal with it well. I'm cool with you being straight with me; you didn't call back because you were with your nigga. And that's cool. I'm all man, baby girl. I'll respect your situation until I no longer give a fuck!" I got closer to her, and she kept her eyes on me this time. I appreciated what she did for me, but I also didn't want this shit to get complicated. Complications could get toxic, and my toxicity could become deadly.

She shifted on her feet, glancing around before locking eyes with me. "You wanna get out of that cell for a little while? I want to show you how much I missed you."

I lifted my chin slightly. "You sure about that?"

"All I can think about," she said, checking her surroundings before unlocking my cell.

Nia didn't wait for me to respond; she just turned and walked off. I waited for a few minutes and eased my gate open. The dude across the way saw the interaction and smiled when I walked out of the cell. He didn't say shit, but he nodded. I guess he knew what it was. I wasn't trying to draw attention, but those around me were going to see it, so it is what it is. I stayed put for a few seconds, letting her get ahead before stepping out. I moved casually, not trying to draw attention, as I made my way to the phone area where she was already waiting. She glanced back at me once before slipping into a supply room.

Following her in, the room was dimly lit, cluttered with supplies and shelves. But shorty didn't look like she was here for a seat. She turned to face me, her eyes on mine, and before she knew it, my lips were attached to hers, and my tongue was down her throat. We hungrily attacked one another; all I could think about was being inside of her.

"Do you have a condom?" I asked between kisses.

"Yes." Hearing her say that was all I needed to hear.

I pulled her into me, my hands gripping her waist, and in seconds, her clothes were coming off, and so was mine. This wasn't a love-making session, but I promise I was about to deliver just what she was looking for. She handed the condom to me, and I had to chuckle because baby girl was on a mission, and she knew what she wanted when she approached my cell. I sheathed my dick and couldn't help but to stare at her. This girl is so fucking beautiful. I wasn't sure how we got here, but I had never wanted fuck somebody so damn bad. On top of that, I was in jail, and my damn pussy supply was low. This was so low vibrational, but oh fucking well. Gotta get it how you live it.

"I want you, Javari," she mumbled.

"I'm right here, beautiful," I whispered as I trailed kisses from her lips to her breast.

The moment my fingers grazed her clit, she let out a soft moan, and that shit was so sexy as fuck to me. Hearing her cries of ecstasy caused my dick to pulsate, and I was ready to gut the fuck outta this girl in this room.

"Please," she pleaded, and hearing her beg caused me to apply pressure and continue to wreak havoc on her pussy.

"Shit," she blurted, grinding her pussy on my fingers, and I knew she was about to cum. Pulling my hands away from her just as her breath got caught in her throat, I chuckled because I knew that breath was her nut about to take over. Lifting her into my arms and pinning her to the wall, I eased inside of her with force, giving her deep thrusts.

"Fuck you feel good," I mumbled, biting down on my bottom lip while gripping her ass as I pushed deeper inside of her.

"Fuck me! Please fuck me," she cried out as she met me thrust for thrust.

Gripping her ass, I began slamming her up and down on the dick and the harder I went, the more she cried out. I was fucking the shit out of this girl, and all she could do at this point was to hold on and get fucked.

"I'm cumming," she moaned, and the minute she tightened her pussy around my dick, I swear my soul left my fucking body and pulled my cum out with it. Once we gathered ourselves, I eased out of her and placed her on her feet.

"I wish that we were in a different situation. I know you may not respect me for pushing up on you in a place like this. I'm just attracted to you." She gave me a half smile.

"Everything is all good." I smiled, kissing her lips as we

grabbed something to clean up with until we got to the bathroom.

Once I got myself together, I made sure the coast was clear and eased out of the room. This was a dangerous game, and I prayed she knew what she was getting herself into because one thing is for sure— I'ma be in that pussy every time she was working and wouldn't give no fucks about that nigga waiting for her at home.

## NIA

My shift was finally over, and I couldn't even lie, I was smiling on the inside like I'd just kissed my high school crush. That man was everything, from his looks to his conversation, and I'm not going to even talk about the way he handled me with his stroke game. Oh my god, he's so damn fine. The first time I saw him, it was like he had me hypnotized. I couldn't look away; it was just something about him that I couldn't shake. I wasn't going to say anything to him, just admire him from afar. But the entire time he was in the cafeteria, he didn't eat.

Trust me, I could understand why he didn't want to eat. It was just seeing him eat and drink water that bothered me, so I shared my dinner with him. I'm not going to lie; I'm so attracted to him, and the more I'm around him, the more my attraction to him grows. I was taking extra shifts on my off days just so that I could spend time with him. I wanted to be near him all the time, but I also thought about him not eating when I wasn't here. I was in too deep, and I knew it. I only had one coworker who knew what was up, and I prayed she didn't tell anyone. At least she said she wasn't going to say anything. This shit was crazy, and I knew I shouldn't have listened to my best friend.

As soon as I got into my car and got my seatbelt on, my phone started ringing. I connected the call to the car, and when I saw that it was my best friend Keisha, I chuckled.

"Hey, boo. What's up?" I answered calmly, trying to play it cool.

"What's up?! Bitch, I will come through this damn phone and smack that dumb-ass smile off your face!" Keisha snapped. "Now that we got formalities and threats out the way. Did you get the jailhouse dick from America's Most Wanted! And before your ass answer that, bihhh, I wanna know everything. If that nigga got lil' fine baby hairs on the dick, I wanna know. If he got a heart on his booty cheek for a birthmark, bitch, I wanna know that shit too," she said, and I damn near choked.

"Keish..." I started, but she was still going.

"Nah...Nah...Nah...I'm not through. You need to know how serious I am right now. Nia, that man is fine as fuck. I'd be a pen pal writing ass fool if that nigga was my jailbird selection. If I was you, I'd be riding dick every two hours of my shift. Ion do convicts, but baby, if the convicts look like that, I'm doing they ass. I'ma be on time for every visitation day, just to sneak and ride dick in the visitation room over by the vending machines. I already got my jailhouse pose on lock. I swear I would risk it all. My job, my freedom; I'd risk Dave's no job having ass ten times over." I hollered because Keisha couldn't stand my boyfriend, Dave.

"Keish, listen—" I tried speaking again, and her ass wouldn't let up. She was still going.

"I saw him on the news when they were taking him into court, and he seemed as if he walked a little bowlegged. Sis, was that the restraints, or was that that mufuckin' pressure? 'Cause, baby, his mama did her big one on him!" I was laughing so damn hard I couldn't drive my car. This girl was a nutcase, and that's why I loved her because she kept me laughing, and when I needed it, she was there for me. She's the reason I got this job because her cousin worked in human resources.

"Okay," I sighed. "I don't like to kiss and tell, but if I die tomorrow, just know God blessed me tonight." I meant every word of that. This man had me gone, and I just got a sample of the dick.

"Bitchhh! You betta talk about it and stand on his word. That's the kind of blessing I need in my life! Oh, hold up, they talking about him on Facebook. Somebody just posted his picture and said that she would donate her uterus to him for experimental purposes. I know that's the fuck right! That Cartel ass nigga can have my uterus, cervix, and ovaries if he want 'em.

Nia, you betta act like you know and be the biggest hoe. Give that nigga a baby expeditiously. I mean, it will probably be walking around with machine guns at two, but it sounds like an interesting life." She laughed, and I was already in a fit of laughter.

"No, she didn't! Not for *experimental purposes!*"

"Yes, she did! The post got ten thousand comments; these hoes want that felon! Oh, shit, wait! Did you know he has a twin?! I just got pregnant. One for you, and one for me! Hannem here!" I swear this girl had me wheezing.

We spoke for a few more minutes and made promises to have brunch on Sunday. I was laughing at my friend, but this was some serious shit because I had a whole damn man at home. Besides that, I'd done my research on him. I knew exactly who his family was and what kind of power they held. I had seen his wife on the news, sitting in the courtroom while the world watched her husband get convicted. I wasn't dumb; I knew better. I knew I shouldn't be messing with a married man, a dangerous man, and an inmate at that. I couldn't stop myself if I wanted to; the worst part was that I didn't want to stop.

By the time I got home, it was a little after midnight. I stopped by Wendy's to get me something to eat because I didn't eat. Walking into the house, Dave was lying on the couch. I hoped he looked for a job today because it was hard trying to maintain these bills by myself. He lost his job two years ago and hasn't been working since. Now he's on this wanna-be street dude, and he can't even do that shit right. I'm so fed up with his bullshit, and not to mention, he's starting to be on some other shit now.

"Hey," I spoke. He stood to follow me into the kitchen.

"Sup, what did you bring us to eat?" He asked, looking into the bag.

"I didn't bring us anything. I got me something to eat because I didn't eat at work. Dave, you've been here all day, and you didn't cook anything?" I looked up at him.

"I've been busy, but that's beside the point. If you get something, yo' ass supposed to get me something too!" He frowned, looking from me to the bag of food.

"When you start showing those same sentiments, then I will because I can't even count how many times you walked in here with food and didn't bring me anything." I spat, grabbing the bag off the counter. I tried walking out of the kitchen, and he snatched my food.

"Nah, you ain't eating this shit if I'm not eating." He dumped my food out, opening it and throwing it in the garbage disposal. I was so sick of this nigga, I wanted to smack the shit outta him.

"What the fuck! Bet. If that's what we're on, I'ma knock all this shit over every time yo' dusty ass tries to eat in my face. You just remember who started it. I'm sick of your ass. This shit right here is getting old, and if you can't get it together, I don't want this relationship anymore," I fussed.

"Shut the fuck up! I'm not going no damn where. Play with me if you want to, Nia." He jumped in my face, and I instantly jumped back, thinking that he might hit me. He's been doing that a lot lately, making me think that he's about to hit me. I've been with Dave for five years, and he's hit me once, and that damn near ended our relationship. He knows if he does that shit again, that's the end of us. I'm not putting up with no abuse shit, and I mean that.

I pushed past him, headed into my bedroom for a shower, and decided to call it a night. This nigga done pissed me off, and all I wanted was to go back to work and climb in the bunk with my piece of calm. That's how it felt when I was near him.

## JAVARI

### *One Week Later*

I'm glad my brother understood why I had to be out for so long. It was imperative that I make these moves to ensure that we have everything we need to move forward. Walking into my parents' home, it didn't feel right knowing my Pop was no longer here. I could hear my mom talking, so I followed her voice. She was in the kitchen sitting at the island, eating lunch, talking to the chef about dinner.

"Son, I thought you were coming over to have dinner with me tonight?" she questioned, standing to give me a kiss.

"Yeah, I need a raincheck on that mom. I gotta deal with Tori and her shit, I asked her to leave my house, and she's still there. The only reason I haven't dragged her ass out of there is because I'm trying to tie up loose ends before I go back inside."

"So, have you decided what you want to do with Ciani? She can stay here while you're inside. I just pray the lawyer can find a way out of this for you." She patted me on my back as Chef Ken placed a plate of fish and chips in front of me for me to have lunch with my mom.

"Have you spoken to Jakari?" I looked over at her.

"Yes, every day. He seems to be alright in there. He said he wanted you to get the operation as you all need it to be. Did your dad have it in a mess?" she asked.

"Nah, you know Pop. He thought we were still back in a time when a conversation, or just the mention of our names and whom we were connected to, might've worked. Times have evolved, mom, and had we evolved with it, I might not have been sentenced to twenty years or even been charged for this bullshit. I'm working on it, and I can promise you that Jakari and I won't be in jail for too much longer.

I'll be needing your help for sure with Ciani, and I've asked Nick to increase security around you until I can get everything situated out here. I've been hearing that the Sandoval's want retaliation over what happened to Ziek. If they want smoke, I'ma give them the whole damn detonator. I just need you and my daughter safe. Maybe you and Aunty need to take Ciani on vacation for a few weeks. The guards will be with you, and it's on me."

"Ok, that's a good idea. I need time away; I'm still trying to process everything regarding your dad," she said to me and then looked away. Something was off, and I needed to make sure she was alright.

"Ma, are you ok? Is everything alright with Pop's estate?"

"Yes, everything is ok. The will is still scheduled to be read next month." She gave a half smile, and I'm not sure if I believed her. I would snap a nigga in two over my mom, I loved my Pop to death, but my mama, my love for her is something serious, and I'll never play about her.

"I'll ask Stephanie our travel agent to see if she can get us a vacation set up to leave in a few days." She grabbed her phone and walked out to go handle that. I sat in silence while I finished my food. My phone started ringing, and it was Jade calling. I brought her a phone so that she could call me if there was an emergency. The warehouse is highly secured, and the cameras are always on out there. But she wasn't being held captive, so having a phone wasn't an issue.

"Yeah," I answered, placing the call on speaker.

"Hey, Javari. Do you mind picking me up some onions, milk, and cornmeal from the grocery store? Oh, and I need some pantyliners; I'm running low. If you need me to text you, I will," she stated, and I swear I had to look at the damn phone like she could see my ass. I haven't been inside a damn grocery store in years; I have fuckin' buyers. Buyers for my groceries, buyers for my necessities, and buyers for my clothes. So, me walking into a grocery store for pantyliners and corn meal was absurd as fuck.

"I got you." I sighed, and she giggled.

"I gotta handle something, so I might not be the one dropping it off."

"Awww, I was hoping to see you. I've kind of gotten used

to talking to you and seeing you daily." Hearing her pout caused me to smile. She was right; I've gotten used to that as well. Ever since the night I found her, I've been at the warehouse every day. I even caught her lil' thieving ass out in my pasture picking some of my weed. I didn't smoke, but lil mama was a damn hoover. I asked Jakari to see what we could find on her, but nothing was coming up because she didn't belong to Forelli.

"I'll see what I can do," Is all I had to say, and I ended the call with her. I knew Milan was on a job, and I had some shit to handle at home. So, I sent Mace a text to go pick up the things for me.

> Me: Bro, I need you to do me a favor. Can you go to the grocery store and pick these items up for me? I need to get onions, milk, cornmeal, and panty liners.

> Mace: Nigga, I sell drugs and smoke weed! I ain't no damn errand boy. I'm high as fuck, and you're about to blow my shit. I can feel it.

> Me: Bro, go get the shit and drop it off to Jade at the warehouse. I gotta handle something right now.

Mace: I know you fuckin' lyin! Nigga, I think I saw her on the missing billboard on the expressway. You know how they have the digital boards and all of the missing people be flashing on there. I think I saw abductee on there. But uhhh yeah, no! Ion do kidnappings, nor do I go shopping off a list she gave the kidnappers. Nigga, y'all need to just give up! She won!

Me: Take the shit!

Mace: Urgghhh! I'm throwing that shit to the gate and driving off. She better take her ass to the road to get it.

This nigga got on my nerve; I just knew he was going to show his ass just like I know he's going to show his ass when I tell him I need for him to fly to Las Vegas with me. About an hour later, I was pulling into my driveway. Tori really didn't understand me when I told her that this shit was over. Walking into the house, our staff was moving around, cleaning, and cooking, and the nanny was even here with Ciani. The nanny said that Tori was upstairs. I asked her to take Ciani and head over to my mother's house. That was nothing unusual for her to do because when Ci was over there, she would always go there with her. I sent all of the staff home, and I waited for everyone to leave before I headed upstairs.

It's crazy because being here in this house hurts the fuck

out of me. This was my place of peace, and now all I feel is pain. I loved this woman. She ripped my heart out and spit on that shit, and for that, I can't forgive her, and this bitch gotta go. I'm not killing this dirty bitch because she decided she wanted to cheat, but I'ma make her feel like she'd dead, and that's on my mama.

Walking off of the elevator and heading into my bedroom, she was lying on the bed naked. She knew the moment I pulled up that I was home, and I hoped her pregnant ass didn't think I was ever going to crawl back into some pussy that another nigga done laid in. Placing the papers on the dresser, I leaned against the wall with my gaze on her.

"Baby, please don't throw us away. I made a mistake, and I know I should've waited for you. I was just lonely, Jav. I'm so sorry." She stood from the bed and attempted to approach me, but the moment I pulled my gun and placed it on top of the divorce papers that I had drawn up on the dresser that I was standing beside halted her steps.

"I asked you to get the fuck out of my house, and that's what I meant. I'm not going to ask you again; put some clothes on and get the fuck out. Oh, and when you're putting their clothes on, make sure it's a pair of tights and a T-shirt. Everything in that bitch I paid for, and you won't be leaving here with any of that shit. Get the fuck out! And before you go, I'ma need you to sign those papers. You will walk your ass out of this marriage the same way you walked the fuck in,

BROKE!" I gritted in her face because this chick was pissing me off with these crocodile ass tears.

"Jav, we can't do this to Ci. She's going to miss being here with her dad." She cried.

I chuckled. "She's going to be here with her dad. You're not taking my daughter with you. I'll let you see her, but that's as far as this shit goes. The only reason I'm doing that is because I truly don't want to hurt my daughter. Now you have ten minutes to sign these papers and get the fuck out of my shit or I'ma drag your ass out!" I roared, and she jumped.

"Jav! Please, you can't take my daughter! You can't do that, please! I'm begging you!" she screamed.

"You fucked up, not me! My daughter stays with me!" I was tired of going back and forth with this chick. She grabbed some clothes out of her drawer and threw them on.

"Sign the fuckin' papers!"

"I can't!" she cried, and I pulled her to me by her damn neck.

"Don't fuck with me. I'm trying my hardest not to kill you, but you're pushing it. I want nothing more than to pull this fuckin' trigger and drop your disloyal ass. Sign!" I gritted.

"Ohhh God, Jav. I'm so sorry! She's not your daughter!" She screamed, crying uncontrollably.

"I'm not giving you her because she's not yours!" she screamed, and I stepped back. My heart felt like this bitch just ripped it from my chest and threw that shit in the trash. What the fuck!

"What did you just say?" I asked because I needed her to repeat herself.

"Jav, I'm sorry. Please! Oh God, please forgive me." She sobbed, her voice trembling with fear. My grip tightened around the gun, the steel pressing against her forehead. My vision blurred, and I saw red. Tears burned my eyes, and rage filled me to the point of no return. The tears that I tried to hold began to fall, and I didn't give a fuck.

That was my baby girl. My whole world. And to find out she wasn't mine had me ready to burn this city the fuck down. My breathing was ragged, my chest rising and falling so fast I could barely think. My trigger finger twitched. It would be easy as fuck to pull the trigger.

*Pull that shit, nigga. It'll all be over if you just pull the muthafuckin' trigger.*

"Urggghhhhhhhhhh, FUCK!" I jerked the gun away and emptied the clip into the wall. My body rocked with anger as I cried out, and this bitch just stood there shaking and crying like somebody hurt the fuck her. I was fuckin' broken. I gave this woman everything. My loyalty. My name. My love. My Money. Freedom to do whatever she wanted to do in life and this bitch chose to be a disloyal hoe. Cheating was one thing. Getting pregnant by another nigga is something totally different and the cause of my raft! But letting me go years loving a child, thinking she was mine, when you knew all along that she wasn't my kid is fuckin' diabolical. Pulling my other gun from my waist, I gripped her up.

105

"Sign the fucking papers, or I swear I'ma pull this bitch and splatter your brains all over this muthafucka and make it my personal wallpaper. I don't give a fuck that she's not mine. That's my fuckin' daughter, bitch, blood or not!" I roared. She signed the papers, and when she was finished, I dragged her ass out the front door kicking and screaming..

Rushing back inside, I went to look for her purse. I pulled all of her credit cards out, leaving her driver's license inside, and threw that shit out the door with her. She was still lying on the ground in tears. The only thing her ass was leaving with was regret. Fuck her!

I called her an Uber, and when they showed up, I gave him an extra hundred dollars and told him to take her where she needed to go. I just wanted her off my shit, and I told her if I ever saw her again, I was pulling my shit and killing her. I'm not even sure if I'll let my daughter see her again. Fuck them people! That's my fucking baby girl, and I'll kill anybody that says anything different. My name is on the birth certificate, and anything my words don't solve, I can guarantee my muthafuckin' clip will.

I pulled a bottle of my *Reserve Bar Louis XIII Black Pearl* from the bar and poured myself a drink. Rage filled me, and I felt like I was about to erupt. I tried not to drown myself in alcohol, but all I could think about was how my family was ripped apart without notice. Rage began to take over, and I lost it.

Everything in my sight, I tore the fuck up in this house. I

felt like I was losing my damn mind. Everything that she decorated in here was destroyed. Every painting and every family photo was on the floor destroyed. The only pictures that remained were those of my daughter. I sat here for hours as thoughts of my marriage ran through me. Something tells me this bitch was playing me the entire time.

---

It was a little after eight, and I had to get out of here. It was too much just being in this house. Downing my drink and grabbing the bottle off of the counter, I headed out to the garage. I sped out of the driveway and hit the highway. It took me about an hour and a half to get out to my warehouse because of traffic. I decided not to go near Jade because I didn't want to let my aggression out on her accidentally. I went straight for the gun range, this place always helped me calm down, and it damn sure helped keep the murder rate in the city down. Turning on the music and placed the glasses over my eyes. I grabbed my gun and let that shit rip. I was down here for about an hour, and the more I drank, the more pissed I became.

"Fuckkkkkkk!" I roared, lifting my gun and emptying my clip again. Tears fell from my eyes just thinking about Ciani not being my daughter. That shit made me feel like somebody came and snatched my air supply from me. *Love Scene by Joe* started playing, and I swear if I were close enough to the speaker, I would stomp a mudhole in that shit. I couldn't see her, but I felt her presence. She didn't say anything, but I knew she was in the room with me, and if she knew like I did, it was best that she left.

Her hand slid across my back in a circular motion, and before she could move, I pulled her in front of me, and she was now pressed up against the gun table.

"It might be best that you leave." My eyes were heavy, and my voice was filled with emotion, mixed emotions.

"What if I don't want to leave?" She whispered.

"I won't be responsible for what I'll do to you in here. Jade, it's best that you go somewhere that's safe. I'm not safe right now." Our lips were so close I could feel her warm breath tickle my nose. If she puckered her lips, they would be on mine, and I swear I wasn't letting up off them muthafuckas.

"I'm a big girl, Javari. I love living on the dangerous side." She slid her tongue out onto my lips, and I tried to suck them off her damn face. Our kiss was so damn aggressive I wasted no time pulling our clothes off. I damn near ripped her shit off, and my God, this woman was breathtaking. I knew it was too soon for some shit like this, but we were at a point of no return. I couldn't promise her shit because I knew it would be a long time before I could trust another woman, especially having a woman in my private space.

"Let's think tomorrow. Tonight we'll live in the moment," she said, pulling me out of my thoughts. She wrapped her arms around me as I nibbled and sucked on her neck. My fingers eased between her legs, and I began massaging her clit while sucking her nipple into my mouth, giving both breasts equal attention.

"Oh fuck!" She cried out. Lifting her up and placing her on the bench, I spread her legs apart, and I tried easing in her, but I got a little resistance. For a minute, I thought Shorty was a virgin by the way she was moaning and trying to run from the dick.

"Is this your first time, beautiful?" I had to ask her because if it was, this was about to end.

"No, I just haven't had sex in a long time, and you're pretty big in size. Please don't stop, Javari." She whimpered because the head of my dick was still inside of her. Pulling it out, I began rubbing my dick up and down her slit, and the sensation damn near made my knees buckle. She was wet as fuck, and my dick was hard as fuck. Baby girl was in trouble, and I loved that shit for her. I eased inside of her, and even though I felt the resistance, I pushed in, and tears fell from her eyes as she cried out.

"Please," she begged and whimpered. I let out a breath that I didn't even know I was holding. I began moving in and out of her with ease, trying to allow her time to adjust to what I was giving her. I'm not going to lie; this pussy was gold, and I've never had pussy suck me in the way that she was doing; the shit was crazy.

"Fuck! This some dangerous shit between your legs,

beautiful," I growled, picking up the pace as my thrust deepened.

"Oh, God. I'm about to cum!" She screamed as she held on for dear life because I was shredding the fuck out of this pussy. My strokes became more intense, and the more I deep stroked her, the more her pussy started gripping my dick. It was like it had a mind of its own, and baby girl had no control over what was happening to her. Shorty was losing it, and I loved that shit.

"I gotta pee, Javari," she moaned, and I spread her legs apart, gripping her ass, and tore her ass up.

"That's not pee, beautiful. Just let go, and let Jav, baby," I told her as I pounded on her g-spot. Seconds later, she erupted, squirting so hard her head fell back, and she didn't seem like she was moving. And just as all of that was happening, I was cumming.

"Ohhh, shit," I growled. Shorty wasn't moving, and I pulled out of her.

"Jade!" I started shaking her. Then I went to grab a cold rag and place it over her head, and she came out of it.

"What happened?" she asked, looking up at me, and I chuckled.

"You let a real nigga inside of you." I shook my head, lifted her into my arms, and carried her up to the apartment. For the rest of the night, lil mama and I got more acquainted. Something was telling me that it was going to be hard staying away from her, but I damn sure had to try because I didn't want her getting caught in some shit that I wasn't ready for.

---

A COUPLE OF DAYS PASSED, and we were on our way to Las Vegas to meet with Draius Chandler. This meeting was very important, and if it goes the way I hope it does, this could elevate the Taleo Cartel to higher heights.

"I can't believe you wanna take flights right now. It's too many damn planes crashing, and ion wanna be the next one. I need to go ask your damn pilot how long his ass has been flying. We should've told Chandler ass to come and meet with us. It's a safer and more reliable way to stay alive. After this, I'm not flying anymore, not until next year. If I die, I swear I'ma beat yo' ass from heaven to hell. Milan was laughing so hard she was choking, and all I could do was shake my damn head. This nigga was definitely touched.

Our flight was a little over five hours, and we landed about thirty minutes ago. We were pulling up to the location that Chandler's people sent me. Once we made it to the restaurant, we headed inside. My security was limited because we were traveling, but best believe I was still deep with it.

The air was thick, the lights were dim, and the smell of cigar smoke was strong. There sat Draius Chandler, the head of the Chandler Cartel. I exhaled slowly because I knew how important this was, and I didn't want to mess this up.

Mr. Chandler, I'm Javari Taleo. It's good seeing you, sir." I greeted, as we approached the table.

"Javari, it's nice to see you again. I'm sorry to hear about the passing of your father. Even though we couldn't do business together at the time, he was still a good man. And I'm sorry to hear about your troubles; I see that you've made some arrangements to be here. I won't dare ask you how that happened, but you must know that I'm impressed."

He leaned back in his chair, swirling a glass of tequila in his hand. Across from him sat his nephews, Marco and Ramone. It was something about these dudes that didn't sit right with me. I made a mental note to look further into them. A deal needed to be made here today; this could be the most powerful shift of power the underworld of cartels has ever seen.

"You asked for this meeting, Javari. Tell me, what can The Taleo Cartel bring to my table that I can't bring myself?" he smiled.

"Opportunity. I know that you're looking for ways to make sure your money is cleaned and that you can move it in and out of the US as needed. As you know, Taleo, we own some major lucrative businesses, such as casinos, clubs, and resorts. We've created a system that would impress the banking industry, so I know it would impress you. With my access, your money moves, and with your access being as though you have two of the largest ports in the world. That would ensure that our weight moves. If we join forces, well, that's the recipe for good business. No more delays coming through the ports, and our distributions will be smooth.

"I'm not sure I'm convinced that this is a good deal." He leaned up in his chair; he didn't look well, but I wasn't a doctor, so that wasn't my concern.

"Listen, your organization is strong and powerful but without stable finances. It's not enough to keep your house from falling. In reality, you have the money; I know what type of power you have, but what good is all that money if you can't clean it? Let us bridge the gap. Our accountants can start accepting your money through our ports as soon as next week. Just as long as I can start pushing my weight through your territories without crossing paths with you. That's a win across the board.

He zoned out, deep in his thoughts. Forming an alliance means loyalty and trust. Can I trust you to hold up your end of the deal? I can give you all of the access you need, but will you be able to handle what comes with that? Can your men handle trouble when it threatens our foundation?" He asked.

"Loyalty is what I stand on. And my men can handle anything that comes our way. Just as long as you got me for what I need, I got you. I will have enough men transporting your money, and if anybody comes for it, well, they gonna have a hard time leaving the way they showed up. Chandler nodded slowly; I knew he was heavy in thought, and if he needed to think about this shit, he could. But I needed an answer by morning. Expanding our reach could be a game changer, and I was ready to make some moves. He stood from his seat, extended his hand, and I stood to shake it.

"We have a deal." He smiled.

"We're about to make a lot of money together. I'll have my people send something over for you to review. Now that we're in business together, how deep are you in with the feds and local and federal judges?" I asked him. I think we have enough to try and get you what you need." I was happy as hell to hear him say that. These are the moves that we're supposed to be making. This allegiance is a power move, and now the Taleo Cartel has just leveled up even more. I know my dad is smiling down on us right now, proud of what we're doing in such a short time. Just as I was walking out of the meeting, I got a text from Jade.

> Jade: Hey, I haven't heard from you in a couple of days. I hope you're ok.

> Me: Sup, beautiful. I'm away on business, but I'll stop by to see you soon.

> Jade: Ok.

Her response was short, but I shrugged it off and didn't even bother to feed into it. I didn't want her to think that because we had sex, that I was pulling back from her. I just had to handle this business. Not to mention I had to go back inside so that my brother could have a break from that shit. I have to handle this shit with the judges quick, but I need to know who's going to be handling my appeal hearing first. Hopefully, we'll know something soon. For the next few days, I handled some business and made sure that my mom, aunt, and daughter got settled on their vacation in the Dominican Republic. I *can't wait by Shaun Milli* started playing, and I had to chuckle at the thought. I'm not sure what my plans are with my compound yet; there are so many memories there with something that I thought was real. I spent some time at the warehouse with Jade, and I wanted to be honest with her, so I told her what it was with my marriage. It was one of the deepest conversations I've had with a woman in a long time. I've always been a man of my word, and I didn't want to give her any false hope. She said she understood, and I hope that was the case. I enjoyed spending time with her, and I damn sure enjoyed crawling between those thighs. Jade was a beautiful woman; I just needed to know what she had going on so that I could help her. I couldn't tell her anything that I had going on with the business or me going back to prison, so I told her I had to go away on business and that I'd be gone for a while. She nodded, but not sure she believed me.

Today was the day I was walking inside the Pennsylvania Federal prison to visit my brother. One thing about Javari Taleo, when I come up with a plan, it's going to always be one for the books. Seeing my men running this entire visitation process made me smile; we'd infiltrated the prison system, and I didn't feel bad about coming back inside. Everything I needed was behind these walls. I even had it set up so that I wouldn't be on the same block as the general population. It was going to take a few days to set that up. But when it happened, I would be in my own space. I gave the guard my ID, and he pretended to scan it and allowed me to enter the visitation room. I sat and watched the movement of the cameras it does a one-eighty scan of the room. A few minutes later, a guard came and unlocked the bathroom and nodded in my direction. I waited for the camera to do its spin and watched my surroundings before easing into the bathroom. An orange jumpsuit was already inside the bathroom, and I hurried and undressed so that Jakari could change quickly. I placed his wallet and keys on top. He was bringing his burner phone out with him, and mine would already be in my cell waiting. Once I finished dressing, I stood in the bathroom and waited. Ten minutes later, Jakari eased inside, and I had to say I missed the fuck out of my brother.

"Damn, it's good to see you bro." He dapped me up and gave me a brotherly hug.

"Same. I got a great deal done, and you shouldn't have any problems. I gave you the breakdown of everything last night. We'll be switching out in a month. Hopefully, that'll be our last switch. My attorney said we should have an appeal date in a week or so.

"Bet." He started putting the clothes on, and after we

spoke for a few more minutes, he eased the door so that he could watch the camera, and when it was clear, he eased out and entered the waiting room. I waited for a few minutes and followed the same process. Even though our people were working in the visitation room and cameras, it was only done on certain days. We don't know who will access these recordings later. So, we still have to move with precaution and pay attention to detail. I walked out and took a seat at the table, and after Jakari and I spoke for a little while longer, he got up and exited the waiting room. And just like that, we'd traded places.

## JADE

***One Week Later***

I COULDN'T BELIEVE how quickly things had shifted in just a few weeks. Sleeping with him was never part of the plan and catching feelings for him was the furthest thing from my mind. But yet here I am, driving myself crazy just thinking about him. It had only been a little over a month since meeting him, yet I found myself craving him in a way that I couldn't explain. He had this way of being both gentle and aggressive, making me lose myself in every moment we shared. Even though passing out during sex had scared the hell out of me, I was willing to let him take me there every damn time. That's how deep I was in this, and it seemed as if he didn't give a fuck about it.

Now, it felt like he had just disappeared. I felt like something wasn't right about that, but I couldn't be sure. I'm never chasing a man, so if he didn't want to be bothered, that's all he had to say. I knew I wasn't supposed to be here, but I had to stay until I could figure things out. I didn't know who to trust, so I couldn't really talk to Javari or Jakari about it. I didn't know if someone in my family was involved, nor did I want to call my friends until I knew for sure. Someone ordered this kidnapping, and I even overheard him saying that an order to kill me had just taken place. So, on some real shit, I'm happy as fuck that they took me from Forelli. He would've eventually killed me. My life has definitely been turned upside down, and I wasn't stupid. I knew that whoever did this to me was affiliated with my father and his illegal dealings. They had an artist come in to make me look beaten, bruised, and bloody. They asked me to close my eyes and be still while they took pictures. At first, I put up a fight because they were really trying to convince someone, and I could only assume it was my dad. But after their threats to kill me, I cooperated. I did what I had to do to survive.

It's been a week since I've seen Javari, and I've only talked to him twice. I'm in my feelings real bad, and being here isn't helping me. In fact, it's driving me crazy, and I just can't do it anymore. Every memory is of him; he's had me in every position all over this apartment, and I was for sure loosing my mind. I never thought a man or the way he fucked me would have me acting like this.

That's some crazy ass shit, and I just couldn't deal with that anymore. I needed to get home to see my father. I didn't know how he was feeling and how much more time we had. Javari had given me a credit card a few weeks back, and I had tried calling him for the last few days to see if I could use it, but he didn't answer. I didn't have any ID and no way to access my own money, so I had no choice but to use his card to hire my own private security team. I needed protection, and I needed it now. I couldn't trust my father's security team right now. I was with my guards, who had been protecting me for years, but yet I'm abducted under your watch. I know I might be overreacting, but oh well, I'm mad fuck it.

The team of five guards was already here waiting for me, and I was still placing my things inside a duffle bag that Javari had in his closet. My mind was racing. So much had changed too fast. I was caught up with the life that I once had and the life that has become my reality. I knew that whoever was after me was still out there lurking and waiting for the right time to make their move on me again. I couldn't let that happen. I looked at my phone again, contemplating if I should try and call him again. I tried to tell myself that he was busy and that he wasn't my man. He told me what it was, and I guess when a man tells you what it really is, you need to believe him. I could kick my own ass to let some niggas dick, wear my ass out like that and drive my ass insane. That's some crazy work right there. I don't wish this shit on anyone else. I had packed as much as I could; the rest I would have to leave. I grabbed the gun that Javari gave me and placed it inside the duffle, and left the phone on the table. I didn't want anyone tracking my whereabouts. Just as I opened the door, Jakari was coming up the stairs.

"Well, look at you. Where the hell have you been? It's been a minute." I asked with a smile. It was good to see him, but damn, he reminded me so much of his brother, and that put a frown on my face.

"I've had some business to handle, not to mention my father died, so that put me in a bad space. I'm sorry I kind of left you out here to fend for yourself. But what's up? Who are those guys out at the gate? No one is supposed to know about this location," he said to me, and I sighed.

"I know, but your brother said I could leave. So, I thought I could leave at any time. Back then, I wasn't ready, but now I need to get out of here. I'm sorry, I have your number, and I promise to keep in touch. I tried to reach out to your brother to let him know I had to hire those guards. As soon as I'm home, I'll make sure the money is sent back to him." I said, not realizing that I said it with so much attitude.

"Whoa! What's up? Did my brother do something? I know he can be a little uptight, but he doesn't mean any harm." Jakari pulled me back inside with concern on his face.

"I'm good on him; just let him know that I'll send him his money back. I'll be in touch with you, and thank you for everything." I leaned in and kissed his cheek. I really did appreciate Jakari. Because, in the beginning, I was scared as shit, and he ensured my safety.

"Take care of yourself, Jade," he said to me. I nodded and

headed for the door. I met my security team, and Angel Martinez was the head of security. He told me that he would be with me at all times. I gave him everything that I knew about my abduction, and I even warned him about my suspicions of my cousins. Angel had connections, so he was able to secure a flight that was leaving in an hour. It was on a private flight, and he paid for it, and I'd promised to pay him as soon as we got to Las Vegas. Las Vegas has been my home all of my life, but if anything ever happened to my father, I would be packing my things and relocating. I'm not sure where as of yet, but I definitely had to go. It was a quick flight; five hours later, we were on the ground, and a car service was waiting for us. Once we made it to my father's compound, security immediately called the main house to have my father come out to the gate. That's the only way I would enter the gate if my father was escorted out to meet me and ride back to the house with me.

"He's on his way ma'am," The guard stated, and we sat and waited. Ten minutes later, my father and his trusted guard, Jessup, were driving up to the gate, and when they got out of the car, I jumped out.

"Dad!" I ran into his arms, full of tears. I was so happy to be reconnected with my father. I hate that I stayed away so long.

"Ohhhh, my God! I thought you were dead. I don't understand; there were photos of your death." He cried leaning up against the car. "I can't believe you're alive, my beautiful daughter. I'm so very sorry that you got caught in my bullshit! I promise you I will find out who did this to you." He touched my face, and that's when I noticed that he was frail; his eyes had sunken in. He had oxygen attached to him, and I didn't even notice the nurse standing next to him.

"Dad, how bad is your health? Oh god." I cried and felt bad that I made him get out of bed.

"I'm so glad to see you home, Ms. Jade. But we need to get him back inside and into bed. We'll definitely get down to the bottom of what's happened to you," Jessup said to me, and I introduced them to Angel and my guards. I told my dad that I felt the safest having them with me, and he understood. Once we got back to the house, I sat and talked to Jessup and my dad about my abduction and who I was with. My father ordered Jessup to deal with Forelli. I decided not to mention Javari, and Jakari Taleo because I didn't want him to do anything to them. My father acted before thinking some-times, and just the simple fact that they kidnapped me would give the same result. I didn't say anything about my cousins because I wanted Angel to do some intel on them and keep a close eye on them.

"Jade!" Ramone ran into the room, pulling me in for a hug, and I felt uneasy as fuck. It was something up, and I knew they had something to do with this. I would bet my entire inheritance on it. I didn't stay at the house; I stayed at a private location, and I didn't even tell my father where it was. A couple of days passed, and I planned to spend all my time with my dad because they said his time was near. I tried my best to stay away from my cousins, but they lived here, so it was hard to avoid them when I visited. They tried so many times to find out where I had been all this time and where I was staying now.

"Jade, I think it's best that we keep our guards around you. We don't know these guards, and until we find out who had a hand in this, I need to know where you are. Uncle Javier wants us to leave it alone, but you know that's not in me. I gotta protect my only cousin." My cousin Marco said, walking into the kitchen.

"I'm fine with my security," is all I said to him, and it was the look that he gave with this devious ass smirk on his lips.

"Cuzzo, you know Unc isn't getting any better. We gotta be ready for when he takes his last breath. I need to make sure that the business keeps moving; I think you should let me and Ramone continue to rock out with the Cartel, and you can just sit back, collect your money, and stay fine," he said with a smile, and I was disgusted; the fuck was he on?

"That's not something I want to discuss right now," I told him. I still haven't heard from Javari, and I had no plans to even call him again. I was able to send Jakari his brother's money back by courier. He tried to decline it, but I wasn't taking no for an answer. He finally gave me an address where I could send the money.

I was making my dad some of my special eggs to see if I could get him to eat. He had started declining day by day, and now he was barely eating. Watching him like this broke my damn heart, and I truly didn't know what I would do without him. I never met my mom because she died giving birth to me, so my father was all I knew. I needed him with me never did I think we would be going through this.

# JAVARI

IT'S BEEN a little over a week, and things are coming together nicely. It seems that the warden was having a little amnesia as to why he's forced to do what the fuck I say, so I had to go remind the nigga. My bodyguard, Nick, was the C.O. on duty today, so he escorted me over to cell block D.

"Jones!" Nick called out as we walked up to his cell.

"Wha...God damn! Please, lawd, please let this fine-ass man be my roommate. I'll die a happy bitch. You fine as fuck, point blank and muthafuckin' period! Do you know I'll suck yo' dick and call you zaddy every night?" I almost punched this fruity ass nigga through the wall, talking that shit to me.

Nick pulled his gun and handed it to me, and this nigga hit the floor and slid under his bunk. That's how skinny his lil' punk ass was. I couldn't even take this hideous nigga seriously with these fuckin' ponytails in his hair. The warden needed his weird ass beat for fucking this nigga. Damn, he couldn't pick a better looking gay nigga, the fuck?

"Nigga calm all that girly shit down and act like a muthafuckin' nigga. What's up with you and the warden?" I asked him.

"The warden! Why you wanna know? Mmm-mmmm, a bad bitch never tells who's dick she's sucking," he said, and I stepped closer to him.

"Okkk...Ok, I suck dick on Monday, Wednesday, and Friday. On Saturday, I work in the bookstore, and Sunday, I repent from all the dick I sucked in the week. Lawd, I'm going to hell, I know. The warden is my boyfriend on Wednesdays. He did everything you thought he did." He smiled.

"You got proof?" I asked him.

"You betta know I do because baby, you not about to play with me. That's why I get my way around here." He smiled, twirling his ponytail.

We talked for a few more minutes, and he pulled out his burner phone and sent Nick the video of him and the warden. We already had pictures, and those photos got us this far, but the warden was definitely trying to change up on us, so the shit Dondre had was so much better. Not to mention I had his confession of them being fuck buddies. I promised to put something on his books, and we left the cell and headed down to the warden's office.

I walked right past his secretary and walked into his office. This nigga really had a problem because he was in here getting head from this C.O. that worked here. Thank God it was a chick, but this nigga was nasty as fuck. What the fuck was really going on in this damn prison? The girl fixed her clothes and ran out of the office.

"They really need to throw your nasty ass under the jail, and to make matters worse, these muthafuckas that work for you know your ass is fucked up. I asked for my cell upgrade, but I'm still in general population. I want my shit. You got two days to put it together, and everything I asked for needs to be in it when I get there." I gritted.

"Mr. Taleo, I can't possibly get that for you, and people around here not ask questions. Your men don't run the whole prison. It's going to be hard," he said, and I chuckled. Nick pulled the phone out and started playing the video of Dondre Jones, and fear washed over him.

"Did you think I was playing with you? I thought that we were on the same page when I first approached you, but I see that you need a little more reassurance. Bitch, I will turn your world upside down and destroy you. I'm never to be fucked with," I told him.

"Ok, give me a few days." He held his hands up, and I was satisfied.

"Oh, and another thing, I need to move freely between these blocks. So, Nick here has a list of your crooked ass CO's. Those are the ones we need working these blocks with my men. They need to know who I am and what I have on them. Nick has that list as well; make sure you get them in line." Nick handed him the folder, and we left his office and I headed back to my cell. Later that day, a beautiful ass C.O. walked up to my cell smiling from ear to ear.

"Hey, just wanted to stop by and let you know I'm back to work. I hate that it's been almost a week. I'm not sure it was something I ate that got me sick like that, but I'm better now. I appreciate you calling to check up on me though." She smiled, and I was sitting here looking at her ass trying to figure out what the fuck this chick was talking about.

She unlocked my door and walked in to place a container of food on my table. She stepped closer to me and leaned in to try and kiss my lips while rubbing her hands towards my dick. I curved her and jumped up with a mug on my face. I almost threw this chick against the damn cell door. 'Cause what the fuck was going on in here.

"The fuck is wrong with you!" I yelled, and shorty looked as if she was scared and wanted to cry. She rushed out of the cell, and I was pissed the fuck off. I felt violated. I mean, it would be cool if I was looking for some pussy in here, but nah, this not that. I'd been sitting here for the last hour thinking about the incident with ole girl mad as fuck.

"You good, sir?" Nick questioned, walking up to the cell.

"Yeah, I just had a lil issue with one of the C.O.'s she walked into my cell trying to me. Not sure what that was about, but keep an eye on her. She has a mocha complexion and shoulder-length curly hair."

"Oh, you're talking about Nia?" He laughed, shaking his head.

"Maybe you should talk to Jakari. She and him are a little close if you know what I mean," he said, and I looked at his ass with disdain because, nah nigga, I don't. Then it hit me... I just knew that nigga wouldn't do no wild boy shit like that. I know fuckin' better!

"Give me a minute," I told him damn near breaking my fingers dialing Kari's number.

"Sup, bro!" he spoke into the phone, and I had to throw my damn iPods in my ear.

"Nigga, really! Did your ass forget to tell me to watch my fuckin' dick! I know your ass ain't in here hiding the fuckin' DICK with these chicks in here. Nigga, you were supposed to bring your loose dick ass in here, sit the fuck down and not touch shit! All the free pussy in the free world, and you wait until you go to prison to fuck the guards."

"Yo chill! Don't do anything to fuck with her, nigga. I know your mean ass probably fucked some shit up for me. I like her, and shit just happened. You act like her ass is a prisoner in that bitch. She's in the free world, she just works there. And would it have made a difference if I met her at the mall, the club, or a coffee shop? Chill on her. I mean it, Jav." He sighed.

"Nigga, I feared for my dick. She was about to rape me!" I spat with my nose turned in the air. I was disgusted.

"Man, shut yo' ass up. That was some real dramatic shit to say. And I know you're not calling me a loose dick nigga! What the fuck did you do to Jade? I know damn well you weren't in here fucking with that girl? Ohhh shit! You hit, didn't you?" he questioned.

I dropped my head at the mention of her, because I had so much going on in here that I forgot to call her back. I hate to say it like that, but she wasn't at the top of my list to call. Even from behind these walls, I'm working day in and day out, trying to keep our names at the top of the game. It's always when the head of the family dies that these muthafuckas try and come in and take your shit. It never fails, but they got the right one when they tried us.

"Hello," Kari called out.

"Yeah, how is she?" I sighed, rubbing my hand across my face.

"Pissed and gone. The only time a chick starts acting irrational and on the hate train is when a fuck nigga breaks her heart. You better not had fucked with her, Jav. Jade was really cool. Oh, and she spent all your money too. Broke ass nigga!" He laughed.

"Never. She could go on a shopping spree daily for the rest of her life, and I'll never be broke. Puss boy! Did she say where she was going? Do we even know if she's even from Philly?" I threw all kinds of questions his way.

"I think she's from Vegas."

"Does she still have the phone that I gave her?" I asked him.

"Nah, she left it at the apartment, and the number that she's been calling me from is untraceable. Trust me, I tried because she seemed scared. Which is why she didn't want to give us any information. I'm still working on it though," he said to me.

"Bruh, I thought you were this guru of finding niggas. Please don't tell me you lost your touch. I need to know who she really is, and where she is. Make that a priority. I know you're working with just a first name, but I need more. Look into my credit card charges and see what she did," I told him.

"Nigga, I'm the best at what I do. But we took her from Forelli. There is nothing tracing her to anyone else. She hired a security team to protect her; that's what she charged on your card. And before you ask, I've already tried getting information from them. They won't budge.

His name is Angel Martinez, and he has a private security firm in Philadelphia. He's the best of the best, but his clientele isn't listed in any database. He keeps that classified, and rightfully so. Get this, she sent a courier to my house, and he delivered the money she charged on your card in cash. She even sent an extra hundred grand for our hospitality, and she sent me a dozen cupcakes and told me not to share with you.

So, yeah. She's pissed and you fucked her, didn't you? That's fucked up, Jav. How you gon' come in here and just casually slide your dick in a kidnapped woman?" Kari questioned.

"'Cause he nasty, that's how? And he going to jail- oh, I forgot he already in jail," Mace dumbass spoke in the background. I didn't even know his ass was there.

I chuckled. "Why didn't you tell me he was there?"

"He just walked in. I gotta make sure I take my key back from this dude. He don't even knock. Just walk up in your shit like he lives here." Kari laughed and I had to agree.

"I know you niggas not talking about me. See if I come to see you niggas on visitation day. It's crazy 'cause ion never know which nigga I'ma get when I visit. As a matter of fact, keep fucking with me, and I'ma snitch. I'ma tell 'em that you, you, and he's him and yo ass is really the one that killed Ziek and his 'I'ma take the charges ass' is the one that they arrested.

I must say, though. You niggas did your big one on the switch out. I'm impressed because the shit is literally working, but if I had a brother, that nigga gotta do his own time. Ain't that much 'I'm my brother's keeper' for me." This nigga got on my last damn nerve.

"Kari, pull your gun out and shoot this nigga. Do it quick because I don't want my friend to suffer, but he gotta be put down," I told him, and Jakari was in a fit of laughter.

"Put down? Nigga, I ain't no damn dog, wit' yo' ugly jail-bird ass. You know what, Jav? The next time these niggas out here trying to kill yo' uppity ass. I'ma let 'em at least get one shot off in yo' ass before I step in!" he snapped, and I laughed because Mace knew just as well as I did that he'd never let that happen.

"I gotta go. Kari, send me her number and make sure that you make this a priority. I need eyes on her. If she's in trouble, we can't help her if we don't know who she is or where she is." I ended the call, and a few minutes later, he texted me Jade's number. I spoke to her twice, and both times, she was at the apartment. *Why the fuck did she just up and leave like that? Especially when she was so adamant about staying?* I was confused about it all.

I stared at the number for a minute and hit the call button on the phone.

"Hello." Her voice was low and raspy.

"So, you just leave without saying goodbye?" I questioned.

"Seriously? That's what you say after you ignored my call for three damn days? You wasn't worried about a goodbye then, so tell me, Javari, why are you worried now?" her attitude was evident. I was a little confused about that.

"I'm sorry about that. I've been busy, but you act like it's been weeks. Baby girl, it's hard for me to sit on the phone and talk to you all day when I have to conduct business. I told you if you had an emergency and couldn't get me to call Jakari or Mace. You had both of their numbers, so what's wrong, shorty?" I asked her.

"Nothing. I didn't ask you to sit on the phone with me all day. You could've been courteous enough to just answer and say you didn't have time to talk. It's simple. But it's all good. You had to conduct business and so did I. That's why I left," she snapped, and I had to pull the phone away to look at it like her ass could see me.

"Lil mama, please don't tell me you caught feelings? Listen, I tried to be attentive to your feelings by telling you what I was dealing with. I'm sorry that I got you caught up in this. If my life was different, I would absolutely pursue you. You're fine as fuck, beautiful, funny, and you have this air about you that's calming. Almost like the prefect peace to any storm. I would love to get to know you more though, but please don't rush my process. Jade, I don't even know your full name, and you want me to take this seriously?" I asked her.

"I explained why I'm keeping my last name a secret. I don't know who I can trust right now. Please be patient with me on that," she said, and I fucking laughed hard as hell.

"Do you hear yourself? You don't want to give me your last name because you don't know who you can trust? Yet you fell on the dick of a nigga you can't trust! Make that make sense, baby girl." She was pissing me off because that shit made no sense. I didn't mean to hurt her feelings, but I'll never sugarcoat shit for her. The line beeped and she'd hung up on me. Just as I was about to call her ass back, Draius Chandler was calling me.

"Draius, how are you?" I answered the call.

"Not good right now. My health is declining, son. I have cancer and I'm dying. I felt like you should know since we have deep ties. If something happens to me, you will be notified by my attorney of my death and the details of my services. I set these things up so that my daughter and nephews don't have to worry about things like that. I don't want you to worry; my wishes will be airtight and any business deals or contracts that my organization has will stand until it's run its course. I need a favor from you, though. It seems that I have a problem in your back yard and I need it handled."

"Say less. Just need a name." I stood to get Nick's attention.

"Javier Forelli. And this is personal; I need his head. Literally," he stated, and it took me back to the issues my Pop had with Forelli. Not to mention that's the nigga that took Jade.

"Consider it done. Can you give me any particulars on this situation?" I asked him. Nick already had Milan on the phone, and she was listening in on the call.

"No. I just want him dead, and I need him dead before I die." He started coughing uncontrollably, and I could hear the machines beeping in the background. Once he got it under control, I spoke.

"Consider it done. Expect my gift soon." He ended the call, and I grabbed the phone from Nick, so that I could speak to Milan.

"Lan, get this done tonight, and Nick will set up the logistics for Joe to have this package delivered to Chandler. Mention Jade's name to Forelli before you kill him, and see what information he gives you. Make sure you record it for me," I told her.

"Got it." She hung up, and I thought about calling Jade back but decided against it. I needed to let this thing between us settle. I decided to call my mom to see how they were doing.

"Hey, son. Is everything okay?" she asked, picking up on the first ring. It sounded like she was crying.

"Mom, are you crying? Is everything ok with you?" I asked her.

"I'm fine, just thinking about your father and all the years I was married to him and... You know what? Never mind. You have enough to deal with," she said, and that threw me off because I'll never push her feelings to the side.

"Ma, I'm always here for you if you need me. I just wanted to check in on y'all and see how baby girl was doing. I didn't get a chance to talk to her today." I smiled just thinking about her, but every time I think of her, a pain shot through my heart. I still haven't told my mom about Ciani not being my daughter. That shit was going to break her fucking heart. My mom loved the hell out of her granddaughter.

"She's already sleep for the night, son. She had a long day at the beach, eating shrimp and hamburgers." We both burst out laughing because Ciani killed us with damn shrimp. My baby loved herself some shrimp and thought that she was supposed to eat it with every meal. I tried my best to keep that away from her, because even though they were good, it was also not good to eat it every day. My phone beeped, and it was my lawyer calling.

137

"Ma, I gotta take this. I'll call y'all in the morning. Love you." I clicked over before the call hung up.

"Mr. Robinson. Any news on my appeal?" I hope he was calling with some good news.

"Yes, we have a date. Two weeks from now. Your connection inside the courts worked to get that date pushed up. I also have something that I think will work in our favor. The prosecution suppressed some evidence, and the FBI agent on the scene tampered with that evidence. I have proof. There is a video that was never entered into evidence. The first five minutes of the altercation show you trying to step back from the situation.

It shows him spitting on you, and it shows him pulling his gun on you, and then you pulled yours, but when the gun went off, the person recording went for cover, so we couldn't see anything else. That's all we need. I'm going to get you out of there." You could hear the happiness in his voice. He worked hard, and I know that sentence hurt him just as much as it fucked me up. I saw it in his eyes that he would do all he could, but just in case he couldn't, I'ma have that judge in my muthafuckin' pocket as an ace in the hole.

"That's great news, man. I appreciate you for working so hard to get me out of here. You'll always have a job representing me. Do we have a name on that judge?" I asked him.

"Yes, it's Judge Jamison Marcelli. He's been on the bench for the last thirty years. I like Marcelli; he's always been a fair judge."

I'm going to let him rock out and see if he can get this done on his own. But if shit seems like it's about to be a shit show, I'ma have to have a recess and talk to Marcelli. Fuckkk!

In two weeks, this could all be over. I spoke to him for a few more minutes, and after we ended the call, I went to take a shower so that I could go to bed. On my way back to my cell, I saw shorty that was messing with my brother. Her eyes were red as fire like she'd been crying. I pulled out my phone to text my brother.

> Me: Nigga, you need to handle this situation with your girl. Shorty looks like she's been crying. I don't want her to know what's going on, but fix it.

> Kari: Nigga, you were mean to her. You could've stopped her gently. Now she won't answer any of my calls. You know what? I'll be up to see you in a couple of days on the next visitation. I'm coming back inside, and you can run your lil' maniac mean ass around the city and be mean to them niggas. Not her, fuckin' bully!

Man, I lost it. I laughed so damn hard because this nigga was pussy whipped. He was willingly and ready to come back to jail just so he could be near his girl. I needed this laugh for so many reasons. I didn't even respond to his ass. I just laughed myself to sleep.

## JAKARI

I'VE BEEN BACK INSIDE for about two days now and Nia hasn't been to work since I've been here. I tried calling her phone, and she wasn't answering. I was a little concerned but decided to give her some time to calm down. I know how my brother could be, but she needed to know that I wasn't going to let this shit fester for too long. I gotta admit that I'm feeling Nia a little more than I'd like to admit. The first night that I was with Nia led to me fucking the shit out of her every time she breathed in my direction.

The more I entered her, the more my feelings got involved, and I believe she felt the same way. Which was understandably why she felt some type of way about whatever Javari said We've talked about her situation at home, and the more I think about that shit, the more I feel like she's gonna have to leave her dude. I'm not into this sneaking around shit, and I'm damn sure not in the business of sharing my woman with the next nigga. It's crazy how we met, but I'm not ashamed to say what it is.

The gates automatically opened, and it was time for us to go out on the yard or to the rec room to watch television if we wanted to do that. I just got word from the warden that I'll be moving to new accommodation in a couple of hours, so I stepped out just to get some air outside of that damn cell. I'll be so damn glad when this shit was over Jav told me what the lawyer said, and I couldn't wait for that damn court date.

I decided to rock out until the night before the hearing and Jav will come back in to appear in court.

"Jakari, they have your new cell ready. It's on cell block A; it's more of a holding cell that they have over there, and it's away from the other inmates. I think you'll like this setup." My bodyguard Chris entered my cell. I nodded and he helped me gather my things. One thing about my brother is that when he wanted something done, he made that shit happen.

As we headed down the hall, a sharp pain hit my chest, halting my steps. It had been happening for weeks now. Milan joked that it was because I was too connected to Javari, feeling his stress like it was my own. She could be right. I still couldn't believe the shit Tori did to him. I'm still trying to wrap my mind around all the details of that and the fact that my niece wasn't his daughter. I wanted to pull my gun and shoot the bitch myself.

Trust, that nigga she's fucking with is done out here. Javari put the word out for anybody that's allowing that nigga to eat couldn't eat off of our table. All distributions would stop for that specific area. Then we had our people run up in his traps, cleaning out his drugs and money. Normally, we don't step off our thrones for some bullshit like this, but this shit was personal. By the time we're finished with that nigga, he gon' wish that he'd fucked with a different bitch because that slut bitch he got fucked his life up. I guess they gon' be slumming it together. And before we were done, that nigga is gonna learn exactly who the fuck he was dealing with.

When we got down to A block, I wanted to drop my shit and drag her ass down the hall with me. Nia's ass was down here working. So she saw me calling her and she's been here at work. Her ass had to request to be moved, so that she didn't have to see me anymore. She turned to face me, and as soon as we locked eyes, I walked off.

Once we got to my cell, I let out a loud whistle because this nigga made them fix this shit up. There was a 50-inch television, cable, a nice full-size bed with a pillow-top mattress, a microwave, and a small fridge that was fully stocked with drinks and microwavable foods. I could kiss that nigga's forehead when I see him. Damn, I was going to sleep good as fuck tonight.

Once I got my things situated, I walked back out of my cell and went on a search for Nia. I found her talking to one of the inmates, and when he touched her arm, I almost snapped that nigga's hand in two.

"Touch her again, and I'ma break your fucking neck, bitch!" I turned his hand loose and grabbed her arm, pulling her with me. This shit was crazy that she got me in damn prison about to beat a nigga up because of her.

"What are you doing?" she snatched away from me once I pulled her into the closest bathroom and locked the door. Chris was my lookout out, so he would let me know if someone was coming.

"Nia, don't fucking play with me. I've tried to give you time to cool off. I apologize to you for what I did. I didn't mean to hurt your feelings. I was just going through some shit that night." I sighed, looking away from her because I hated to lie to her.

"Why are you apologizing for something your brother did? After I thought about it, and when I saw him later that night, I knew it wasn't you. I knew you would never treat me that way, but I'm pissed because you dragged me into some shit that I could possibly go to jail over, Jakari. All you had to do was tell me the truth so that I can make decisions for my own life. I already messed up because I'm sleeping with an inmate. But to know that you and your brother are trading places is a federal crime.

You're breaking out of jail, and I now know that's what you're doing. I'll never say anything to anyone, but this is too fucking much."

I pulled her into my personal space, and I just held her as the tears fell. "I'm sorry, baby. You're right I should've told you. But there was no way that I could, and I promise you I'll never allow you to be hurt by this. You're not going to jail; I can promise you that. The shit that I'm in isn't for the weak. I'm a powerful man and a deadly one. So, I can understand if you want to stop seeing me and go on with your life."

She stepped closer, and I took that as she wasn't ready to let up off the dick. I placed light kisses on her lips as I quickly removed her clothes. It's been a minute, and I needed to be inside of her. Trailing kisses down to her breasts, my tongue grazed her nipple. Then my hands moved down to her center, and my fingers started massaging her clit.

"Shit, I need you," she moaned and lifted her up, wasting no time entering her.

"Fuck! This pussy wet!" I gritted, slamming into her. It wasn't shit romantic about this; we were straight fucking.

"You tried to keep this pussy from me, Nia?" I questioned, pounding the fuck out of her pussy. All shorty could do was bury her head into the crook of my neck and dig her nails into my back. Every time she tried to speak, I stroked her so damn good her words got caught in her throat. This was a lesson not to play with me about my pussy. Yeah, my pussy. That nigga gotta go.

"Mmmm! Fuck me, baby!" She screamed, wrapping her arms around my neck, and I did just that. Gripping her ass cheeks as our bodies rocked back and forth as my thrusts became more profound and stronger.

"Got damn!" I growled as we both released together. Later that night, I was knee deep inside of her again. We had a lot to discuss, but I couldn't leave her alone, and I damn sure wasn't letting her walk away from me. Lil mama got a problem on her hands, and I'm not waiting long for her to handle her home front. I just might have to take matters into my own hands.

---

## Two Weeks Later

I WAS SITTING in a holding room waiting for court to start, and I couldn't believe Javari missed visitation hours. Chris and I have been trying to get a hold of Nick and Javari, but neither of them has answered their phones. Chris was the guard that transported me from the prison, and we still had hope that we could make the switch. I dialed him again, and he finally picked up.

"Yeah, we're coming down the hall now. I see our guard on the door; y'all come out now. Chris will have to stay with me until this is over. You and Nick can go and take a seat in the courtroom," he said, ending the call.

Just as soon as Chris opened the door, we quickly made the switch. Nick and I walked into the courtroom, and I took a seat next to my mom. Her and my aunt came back from their vacation a couple of days ago. She held my hand and leaned into me. I knew all of this had taken a toll on her. In all fairness, I would've killed that nigga for less, but he deserved to die. I just hate that we had to go through so much behind it.

145

About an hour into the hearing, it became clear that the prosecution was in trouble. They tried but got caught up in so many lies that they had withheld key evidence in my brother's trial.

"Your Honor, I would like to bring my witness, Rashaad Rivers, back to the stand, the gentleman who authenticated the video earlier. My witness has personal knowledge of what occurred on the night in question," Attorney Robinson stated, motioning the witness to come up and take the stand.

Rashaad took the stand and was sworn in again. Attorney Robinson turned his attention toward him. "Mr. Rivers, can you confirm that the video shown here today is the one you recorded on the night in question?"

"Yes, sir," Rashaad nodded. "That's my video."

"Can you tell me why you didn't come forward earlier in the case?" The judge questioned.

"FBI Agent Donavon came to my house and threatened to hit me with some drug charges if I didn't stay quiet. He said no one was going to believe me over a veteran FBI agent. I thought about it because cops were always trying to pin some shit on us... I'm sorry, but it's true. I got scared, so I kept my mouth shut. Until Attorney Robinson found my name on the list of people who were questioned that night and realized I was never brought in for questioning.

Everyone on that list was here as a witness except me. He told me I wouldn't get in trouble, but he needed me to tell the truth. He wanted to know what I saw that night. So, I showed him the video that I had recorded." He shrugged and let out a sigh of release. The judge leaned back to review the evidence and let out a deep breath before speaking.

"I have always prided myself on fairness in my rulings. Mr. Taleo, I want to take a moment to formally apologize for the scrutiny and injustice you've been subjected to. I can assure you that everyone involved in this will be reprimanded and reported to the disciplinary board. Given the over-whelming evidence of misconduct in this trial, I hereby over-turn your conviction, and it's dismissed with prejudice." He slammed the gavel down and we jumped up and celebrated.

We were fucking free. Javari had his head down, and when he finally lifted his head and turned to us, he was full of emotions. Tears streamed down his face, and that was my muthafuckin' brother. That dude was the definition of I'ma Carry Our Family on my back. He went down for me, and if he had to do it, he would've done those twenty years. It's crazy how my dad died behind this. He was stressed over this trial and Jav being locked up like that. Nate Sandavol was in the courtroom with his mom, and he had a frown on his face, staring Javari down. All I know is he better keep that shit over there because he'll end up in the grave next to his brother.

The next morning, we were in the kitchen eating break-fast at our mom's. The family had come over last night and we celebrated Jav being home for good.

"Daddy! I love you. Can we go see mommy now?" My niece Ciani asked her dad.

"Remember what I told you, baby. Mommy had to go away to get better." I felt bad as fuck for my brother because I'm not sure how he was going to deal with that situation.

"What time is the reading of the will?" Javari asked, looking in mom's direction.

"Eleven. We're meeting at Alvin's office." I looked at my watch and it was already a little after nine.

"I'll meet y'all there," he said, kissing Ciani and heading out. Jav is staying here with mom until he decides what he wants to do with the house. Ciani's nanny comes here to help out with her, and that makes it easier on Javari and my mom. We celebrated so hard last night that I forgot to call Nia, so I sent her a quick text.

> Me: Hey, beautiful. I just wanted to let you know I'm a free man.

> Nia: What! Are you serious? Oh my God! Congratulations Javari!

Ohhhhh fuck! I never told lil mama my name wasn't Javari. I should've told her the night she confessed that she knew he wasn't me. Damn, my ass been slipping. I dialed her number.

"Hello. First, let me just apologize, and I hope you're not upset with me. But I forgot to tell you my name isn't Javari. That's my mean ass brother's name. My name is Jakari Taleo.

"It's nice to meet you, Jakari. I understand why it was done and I don't hold that against..." She stopped talking.

"Nia, get the fuck off the phone and come suck my dick!" I heard her nigga say, and the call ended. My anger went from zero to a thousand. I sent her a text because I'm not about to play with this girl.

> Me: Don't make me fuck you up, Nia! I got one better since he want his dick sucked! I'ma cut that muthafucka off and make his bitch ass suck his own dick!

These muthafuckas done pissed me off. About an hour later, I was walking into my Pop's lawyer's office and my mom and Javari were already seated.

"Sup," I spoke and took a seat, ready for Alvin to get things started.

"Hello," a light voice spoke, and we all turned our attention to the beautiful young lady standing at the door with a woman standing behind her. I didn't have to ask who they were; I knew that the beautiful young woman was our baby sister.

"Hell no, we're not doing this shit right here, Alvin!" My mom jumped up.

"Chance, she's included in the will," he said to my mom, and I knew all hell was about to break loose. For one, we haven't said shit to Javari yet.

"Who the fuck is this?" Javari demanded, standing as he tried to calm our mom.

"Is everything okay?" Our sister Zander asked, scanning the room with suspicion.

"You either want all your shit aired out right here, or you take your ass outside. You got some fucking nerve showing your face here." She glared at my Pop's side piece.

Zander's face twisted in confusion. "Wait, wait! Why does my mom have to leave?"

"Zanny, it's fine," her mom said softly, kissing her cheek. "I'll be in the waiting area if you need me." Without another word, she turned and walked out.

"The fuck is going on?" Javari's patience was thin as fuck.

Mom took a deep breath, turning to Alvin. "I need a moment with my sons."

Alvin smiled and stepped out, with Zander following behind him. The second the door closed, my mom looked over at Javari.

"Javari, I found out a few months before your trial that your father was cheating on me and had been for over twenty-five years. Your brother found out while doing his own investigating," my mom told him.

"Yeah, man. I didn't want to tell you while you were battling the trial. You had too much going on. I went to mom immediately when I found out, but she had already known and confronted him. That girl outside is our baby sister, and the woman is Pop's sidepiece," I said to him, taking a seat, and I swear I saw smoke coming from this nigga's head.

Javari loved our pop beyond measure. He looked up to

him and admired him. If wanting to walk in your father's foot-steps was a person, it would be my brother. The shit hurt me, and I have my own feelings and revelations about my father. So, I know he's truly fucked up about it. Javari's jaw clenched, but he said nothing. His nostrils flared; I could see the wheels turning right before me.

"So, all this time this nigga been disloyal to us? He was really out here living a double life and had a whole other family! For twenty-five fucking years! That's damn near all of our fucking life!" His voice boomed, and the room felt like it shook.

"Nah, I'ma get at that nigga. Dead and all, he gon' have to feel me cause fuck him!" He yelled, and my mom stepped in front of him.

"I know how you feel, baby, but let's just get through this so that we can close this part of our lives. I don't and never will fuck with that bitch out there because you can't tell me she didn't know he was married. She knew. Fucked my husband and had his child. But that child didn't have anything to do with their fucked-up decisions. She's innocent, and from the look of things, she knew nothing about you boys," Mom said, and after Jav calmed down a little. Alvin and Zander came back into the room.

"Zander, I'm your brother, Jakari Taleo." I Introduced.

"My brother! What! I have brothers! Oh, my goodness! And you guys are twins. I gotta call my best friend Taris." She giggled, and I smiled, but Javari was over there mean mugging her little ass.

"Tarissss! Look, I got brothers and their twins. They're so cute!" she giggled, moving her phone from side to side, showing us to her friend.

"Your brother's! Babyyyy they fine-fine!" Taris exclaimed.

"Let Brick call me a bitch again, I'ma get my brothers to beat his ass. Girl, it's up now. You can't tell me nothing!" she smiled, and told her friend she would call her back.

"Ok, let's get down to it. We are here for the reading of the will for Vincent Taleo. Chance, he left you a letter, and he asked that you read it in private. Javari and Jakari, your father left you boys, the Taleo empire, and all associated businesses with ten percent of its yearly earnings going to his daughter, Zander Taleo. Javari, he left you a vacation home located in Bali, and Jakari, he left you his vacation home in St. Barts.

Vincent's net worth is 7.2 billion dollars. He leaves fifty percent of that to his wife, Chance Taleo, and the other fifty percent is to be evenly distributed between his three children, Javari, Jakari, and Zander Taleo. All homes and personal belongings that he owns will be awarded to Chance Taleo. He's also set up a ten-million-dollar trust fund for his granddaughter, Ciani Taleo. This concludes the reading of the will for Vincent Taleo.

"Wait! I need time to process this. If he left 7.2 billion, Ms. Chance gets half, and my brothers and I get the other half, does that mean I get a billi?" She asked, looking around the room.

"Yes, but it'll be a little while," Alvin told her, and she smiled so big in excitement. Javari stood to leave, and she walked over to stand beside him.

"Hey, big brother. What's your name?" she nudged him with a smile.

"Javari," he snapped, and that shit looked like it hurt for him to even tell her his name.

"Let's take a picture," she suggested. I walked over to where her and Javari were standing. The look he gave me let me know he didn't want to take this damn picture and I swear I found the shit so damn funny. My brother wasn't feeling being a big brother right now. She pulled her phone out, took a selfie, and the picture was the most hilarious shit I've seen in a minute. She and I were smiling, and Javari's frown was on full display.

When this is all said and done, and things calm down a little, I think we all need to take a vacation. Javari said his goodbyes and left while I stayed behind and talked to Zander for a little while longer. She told me that she was getting ready to go back to school. She was going to med school and wanted to be a neurosurgeon. She was a witty, but a very smart young woman. She asked me why Javari didn't like her, and I assured her that he would come around. There were a lot of things thrown at him, and as soon as he could process them, they would be in a better place. We agreed to make plans to have lunch in a few days. Just as we walked outside, I got a text.

> Javari: Find out who this dude is that's been calling her a bitch.

I laughed so damn hard because that nigga was a softy.

> Me: Ahhh, he's worried about his baby sis. I'm on it, big brother.

I pulled out of the parking lot and decided to head home. I thought about calling Nia, but decided to wait and see if she would call me back.

# JAVARI

A FEW DAYS HAD PASSED, and I'm still trying to wrap my mind around everything that's happened. I can't even express how I'm feeling about my Pop. I feel like our entire life with him was a lie. Like damn man, why the fuck didn't you just leave instead of pretending that you loved and honored our mother. That's the first of all of this, he hurt my fucking mom. I've never seen a woman love, respect, and honor her husband the way my mom did this nigga, and he had to go and do her like that. Nah, fuck that nigga!

Yes, he gave us a great life. I'm a rich man because of him, but I'd rather have my loyalty and self-respect intact first, before anything else. I'm a muthafuckin' hustler. It's in me, and I could've made this bread on my own. When I said he had to see me even in death, I meant that shit. When I said that loyalty is a word that I don't play about, I meant that shit. That's why I'm the fuck out here on the grounds of our warehouse where his ass is buried with a shovel in my hand digging his ass up, with the help of my guards.

I heard someone from behind us driving up. It was Jakari and Mace pulling up on one of our golf carts because even though we have all of these things on the grounds, the funeral home isn't in walking distance. Kari got off the cart, pulled a chair from the back, and took a seat.

"You sure you want to do this, bro?" He questioned.

"You know me, this shit has been on me for three fuckin' days. He gotta see me, Kari," I spat.

"See you?! Nigga ion mean no harm when I say this, but that nigga dead! How the fuck is he gon' see you?

"Sit this one out, Mace," Kari told him and I agreed.

"Sit this one out?! You two niggas clearly need to sit this out. This nigga out here digging up dead bodies like digging graves and moving bodies is his profession. If you asked me, ever since Tori did this nigga in, he's been acting a lil cra-cra. As a friend, I vote to get his ass some help. You know when crazy niggas be around you too long that shit transfers, and since hanging with you niggas, I feel like that happened to me.

Like one day, I woke up, and my nerves was toh the fuck up. I'ma victim; I ain't never smoked this much weed or drank this much liquor in my life," Mace said, and I made a mental note when I pulled this nigga outta this grave to push his ass in it. We finally got to the casket, and my men helped me pull his shit up. Once we got it up, we opened it and I spit on that nigga. His body was already decaying and smelled horrible, and was damn near to the bone but that shit didn't stop me from disrespecting him the same way he'd disrespected our mom.

"All this fucking time, I trusted and loved you! I respected you! Wanted to be just like you, and you go and hurt our family like this. You a disloyal nigga! And to know how you treated my brother is some fuck shit. The fuck did he do to you, but love your wack ass! Fuck you! My only wish is for you to burn in this grave and hell! Pussy ass nigga!" I doused gasoline all over his casket and set this nigga on fire!

"Ohhhh shit! This nigga ruthless as fuck for real! If I was ole man Taleo, I'd show up in yo' sleep, beat yo' ass and take my damn billions back in blood!" Mace said, shaking his head. Jakari grabbed a fire extinguisher off the cart and sprayed it on his ass. Fuck him, he wanted to be cremated anyway. My mom just went against his wishes and put him in the ground because she didn't believe in that. I didn't have shit else to say, and damn sure didn't want to talk about this dude again. Just as I got into the back of my service car, my phone rang.

"Yeah," I answered as I adjusted in my seat.

"Javari, thank you. I appreciate you taking care of that for me. I fed his head to my gators. It was the most exhilarating feeling." Chandler's voice was low and cracky. I felt bad for the man, and I hope he repented of all of his wrong doings so that he could rest in eternal peace.

"I'm glad I could help. Is there anything else you need?" I asked him.

"Yes, there is one more thing." His voice grew heavier, carrying the weight of something he had been holding onto for a long time.

"I've been thinking about this for a while now, and when this is all said and done, I need you to have a conversation with my daughter." He cleared his throat. "She'll be new to this side of the business. I've done everything in my power to shield her from it, but I know that won't last forever. She has a kind spirit, and a beautiful soul, but that kind of purity makes her a target. People will try to use her kindness for weakness, and I can't have that. She has no desire to deal with the family business, and she damn sure won't be forthcoming about her place in it." He coughed but quickly calmed himself before continuing.

"Of course, I have my people in place to protect her. But I believe you are the right person to ensure she'll be okay. I've watched you for years, Javari. The way you think, the way you move should be studied. What you and your brother pulled off with the prison switch was remarkable work." I listened to him intently but remained quiet, yet internally, my mind raced.

"I'm sure you're wondering how I know about the switch," he chuckled weakly.

"Let's just say you're not the only one that's running the warden. I have old money, power beyond your years, and my reach is long. You see, Javari, your father had died, and you were in jail. Take a moment with what I just said. The force behind the Taleo Cartel was in jail, yet the Taleo Cartel was untouchable. Something told me it was another force driving this fine-tuned machine, and that force was you. I vet my people for years before I align myself with them. I don't make business partnerships based on one meeting.

Your father was a great man. He did well in this business, but I always knew he had something special with his sons. Which is why I didn't go into business with him. I know he was disappointed, but it was a business decision to wait. I waited for the right time. I even left orders, just in case I wasn't here to see it through. I knew for some time now that my health was failing me. Those orders were that an alliance with Javari Taleo was a must," he said, and I couldn't believe we were having this conversation.

"With your guidance, my daughter will be able to operate with a vengeance, if she chooses to. If not, I want you to make her an offer. I have nephews, but they've done too much backhanded shit for me to ever trust them with my most prized possession, my daughter and my cartel. I've gone to great lengths to ensure her privacy. Only a few people know she exists. Keeping her safe has always been my top priority. Even in my death, she will be protected." He coughed; this time it was a little more than the times before. I was concerned for the man because he could barely speak.

I exhaled because his request was deep and surprising. "Sir, this is a lot to take in. If you don't mind me asking, what's your daughter's name? If I'm going to work with her, I would like to meet her at some point," I told him. And just as he began to speak again, he went into a coughing fit, and the call went silent.

"Draius! Sir, are you there? Draius!" I yelled into the phone, and eventually, the call ended.

---

## One Month Later

WE'D ARRIVED in Las Vegas and were on our way to the church where Draius Chandler's funeral services was being held at. It's crazy how things went. From my understanding by his liaison, he declined tremendously and passed away two weeks ago. I'm not sure what took so long for the family to have his funeral, but we were here to pay our respects.

"I hope this funeral doesn't last long. Because I can't do all that damn crying and screaming. Shit like that makes me nervous and I be wanting to get high. So, if shit gets out of hand, I'll be in the car. Ohhh, Jav. I knew it was something I meant to tell you. I went into Five Guy's to get me a burger and fries, and guess who the fuck work there flipping burgers. Tori's ass! And you know I showed out on her ass. Lawd, she looks like she money deprived as fuck too. 'Cause look at this damn picture. You know I had to take me a couple. She down bad as fuck. Look at that Party City wig on her head. Boy, you broke her ass down from a private shopper to Dollar General." Mace shook his head, and Jakari held his phone, looking at the picture of Tori bent over laughing.

When our service truck pulled up to the church, it was packed as hell. Every cartel family looked as if they were in attendance. The Chandler Cartel was respected by all, and just about every Cartel in this place tried their hand at working with Draius Chandler. I just couldn't believe that he gave me an opportunity.

"Jav, it looks like some of the leaders from the INC is here. The Hundero family is here as well." Jakari pointed out as we headed inside the church.

"I've always had this question. Why do you niggas have all these damn exotic names? Like them Hundero niggas, they BLACK as fuck! But their name is Hundero," Mace muttered, and I laughed because nigga what!

Services for Draius Chandler was about to begin. We had just taken our seats when his family started making their entrance. My mind was still stuck on the last conversation I had with him and how adamant he had been about me looking after his daughter, ensuring her safety, and guiding her as she stepped into the empire he left behind. My thoughts shifted when she walked in. She wore a black dress, her face partially hidden behind a half veil, she moved with an authority about her. But it wasn't just her presence that turned heads. It was the security surrounding her. There were guards by her side, and in the back of her, you would've thought they were protecting Jackie O. As they got closer, and her face became clearer and familiar, I almost lost my shit and ended this funeral before it started.

"Yo... ain't that abductee?" Mace muttered, but I barely registered his words. I was too busy staring a hole through her ass. Jade was Draius Chandler's daughter? This is some shit for your ass. I couldn't believe he'd asked me to protect and guide his daughter. If he only knew how much guiding I was doing with his daughter. It's funny how the world works. Never in a million years would I have thought she was the daughter of one of the most powerful men in the world.

"I can't believe this shit," Jakari leaned into me. He was just as shocked as I was.

"Damn! Abductee, out here living the life!" Mace shook his head, and we turned our attention to the services. Well, they turned their attention to the services, my attention was on her beautiful secretive ass. So many people spoke about the man Draius was and how he gave the shirt off his back. His nephews were there, and these niggas still gave me bad vibes, then it hit me. The video Milan sent me before she murdered Forelli. I jumped up and walked outside. The moment I got out the door, I hit play on the recording.

*"Who hired you to kidnap Jade?" Milan questioned.*

*He let out a hearty laugh. "They want her dead, and nothing is going to stop them from getting what they want. His own family. They want his spot, and they'll get it." He smiled, and Milan swiped her Machete across his neck and severed his head from his body.*

"Fuck!" I gritted, and just as I was about to walk back inside, the service was over, and they were bringing his body out. I stepped to the side, and she was not far behind his casket, walking out with her guards and cousins.

"Jade," I called low enough for her to hear me. When she turned in my direction, she was surprised to see me. She asked her security to stand by, and give her a moment as she walked over to me.

"Javari, what are you doing here? How did you find me?" she asked confused with red puffy eyes.

"I was in business with your father. I'm here to pay my respects to him. Why haven't you called me back? I've been calling you for weeks?" I asked her with a frown on my face.

"Oh, I don't know, Javari. I just couldn't sit on the phone with you all day, especially when I have business to handle. You don't like how that feels, huh? You call someone and they disrespectfully decide not to call you back." Her smart-mouthed ass had the nerve to smile, and I had to stop myself from the response I was about to make.

"Listen, you need to be careful. I think your cousins had something to do with your kidnapping. Something Forelli said made me put the pieces together. Your father asked me to look after you, to help you. Of course I didn't know I was you because he never referred to you by your name. But he had a long conversation with me and asked me to do this for him. I want to respect his wishes. I got some things I need to check out, but I'm sure it's them."

She exhaled. "I had a feeling it was them, but I couldn't find anything solid to back it up. Anything you have could help when I take this to the police." I shook my head before she could finish that thought.

"Nah, we don't do the folks. I got this. I was about to leave tonight, but now that I've found you, I think I'll stay for a few days. If that's alright with you?" I looked over at her.

"Ok. Don't think I'm going to fall on your dick either." She stepped forward to hug me and walked over to give Jakari and Mace a quick hug before heading toward her awaiting security detail. I let out a deep breath, watching her go. Damn, she was gorgeous. And I missed the hell out of her. She really had the audacity to curve me on some payback shit. No lie, I had been blowing up her phone, trying to find her. Now, I knew why we kept hitting dead ends. Her father had built protection around her, making sure she was completely untraceable. The only reason they got to her in the first place is because it was an inside job.

## JADE

My heart felt like it was going to jump out of my chest when I saw him. I couldn't believe he was at my father's funeral, and finding out that he had business dealings with my dad surprised me. The death of my dad had been so heavy on me. I thought I was prepared for the day that he transitioned, but I wasn't. I can't believe that he's gone. So many memories with my dad, and that's the only thing that brings me joy. I decided not to have a repast, but my aunt Doris had one at her house. Marco and Ramone were pissed that I didn't have one.

They had the nerve to say I was being disrespectful to my dad's business associates. To be honest, I don't give a damn about any of that. They've been pressing me about my dad's affairs and trying to find out where I'm staying. Thank God Angel has been on top of my security. I've hired his company permanently to guard me, and Jessup from my dad's personal team is joining them. My dad trusted him, and so did I.

The timer on my oven went off and I got up to go take my

Chicken parm out of the oven. There are so many things that I miss about being in Javari's apartment at the warehouse, that's drinking his wine, cooking some of my favorite recipes, and smoking the weed. I wanted to ask them so bad did they bring any because I've been buying some here, and that shit is garbage compared to what they have. It was some of the best homegrown I've ever had. Angel came walking into the kitchen, leaning against the wall.

"That smells amazing." He smiled.

"It is so good. It's one of my favorite dishes. Would you like some?" I asked, looking over at him.

"Sure, I could eat," he said, taking a seat at the table, and I sat a plate in front of him. Once I fixed my food, I joined him for dinner. Before I could take a bite of food, my doorbell sounded off, and I'm sure it was security because they were outside of my door.

"I got it," I told Angel and walked over to the door. I swung the door open and my words got stuck in my throat. He looked so fucking good, so got damn fine, and my God, he smells so good. My body shuttered at the sight of him. It slipped my mind that I texted him my address.

He chuckled. "What's up? Are you going to invite me in?"

Clearing my throat. "Yes, come in." I stepped aside to let him enter. When I told him I wasn't going to just fall on his dick, I prayed for my strength because every time this man is in my presence, I'm weak as fuck. All I can think about is the package he's holding. His wife is stupid as fuck. I get she didn't think he was coming home no time soon but got damn I swear I would've been doing those conjugal visits.

"So, what's going o..." His voice trailed off as his gaze shifted past me. I turned to see what had caught his attention and found him staring at Angel, enjoying his food.

"On to the next one, I see." He stepped over to me, invading my space. I'm not going to lie; that shit hurt my feelings. I haven't seen this man in almost two months, and even with me trying to avoid him and regain some of my damn senses, he comes with some bullshit. That one move was enough to make Angel stand to his feet and by my side in an instant.

"If you care about this nigga, you better get him the fuck out of here." His gaze never left mine, and his attitude was evident. I didn't give a shit about his attitude though. He wasn't going to disrespect me in my shit. I was ready to tell him to get the hell out, but instead, I turned to Angel and asked him to leave.

"Angel, I'll be fine." After he hesitated for a moment, he nodded and left. As soon as the door closed, I turned my attention to Javari.

"I know we haven't known each other long, and I'll be honest with you because I'm a big girl and I can admit when things don't go the way I'd plan. It's never happened to me, and I've always said that love at first sight can't be real. How can a person fall for someone that quick? Love comes when you least expect it.

I can't say that I'm in love, but it's true I caught feelings in the short time that we've known one another. I stopped calling you because I needed to check myself, I needed that break to realign myself. I didn't want to go through a heart-break. I've been through that, and I didn't like it." I sighed, trying to keep my composure intact.

"Look, I get it. You're not ready for a relationship. You just got out of your marriage, and I respect that. But this back-and-forth shit between us; I'm not built for that. I've only been in one relationship, and he broke my heart. I don't want to go through that again. That's why I didn't return your call because what was the point? To hear another excuse or another lie? You curved the fuck out of me, Javari. You fucked me, and you dipped. And yeah, I get that that's part of the game. Especially when I know you made it clear on what you wanted and didn't want. My bad for getting caught up. I promise it won't happen again.

Now that I've put it all on the table. Please know that what I do with whomever I decided to do it with is my business. That shit doesn't concern you. Oh, and whatever my dad asked you to do for me, I'm good. I don't need your help. I've never been a choose me type of girl, Javari. We fucked, I loved it, and that's it. For my sanity, I need for it to be it." I felt myself getting emotional, and I knew I had to keep it together.

"I don't want you feeling like I lied to you about anything. Which is why I opened up to you about my personal life. About my marriage. We've had meaningful conversations, shorty. I didn't treat you like a jump off. I didn't dip on you, and I damn sure didn't lie to you. I excluded information from you because certain things about me you don't need to know for your own good. I'll never put you in a situation that will harm you or hurt you intentionally. I'm a grown ass man; I don't do nigga shit. Fucking and dipping is nigga shit. Lying to a woman and making excuses not to see her, that's nigga shit.

When I said I was handling business, that's what I was doing. I'm not a man of convenience; I'm intentional with everything I do. I don't have to tell you what you want to hear just to get some pussy. Pussy drops out of the sky for me on any given day. I'm a selective man, and I don't have a plethora of women on my roster to select from. I was married to a woman that didn't love me, she didn't respect me, and the crazy part is I gave her all of me. So, excuse me for being cautious, especially when I've only been out of my marriage for two damn seconds," he stated, and I felt bad.

"Ok, I'm sorry. I didn't mean to come off rude or insensitive." I apologized because hearing his side put things into perspective a little more. I wiped the tears that fell, and he stepped closer to me.

"You love me, Jade?" I couldn't believe that after all that I said to him, this is the shit he pulled from that.

"You wanna stop fucking me, Jade?" He moved even closer, pinning me up against the wall. My breath got caught in my throat because I didn't want to stop fucking him. I just couldn't handle the aftermath just in case this thing with us went left.

"Javari, please don't do this to me. I'm in mourning," I pleaded.

"Do what? I just want to make you feel good. Don't you miss me 'cause I miss the fuck out of you and this pussy. I need to feel her. I need to see your face when I'm in the deepest part of you. That shit does something to me. I love those fuck faces you make when I push deep. Yes, I want to take things slow, but I can take them slow and still gut you the fuck out, the Taleo way." The look in his eyes told me that I was about to be in trouble, and it was trouble that I welcomed because this man had me too far gone.

He tilted my chin up, his tongue traced my lips, and my body shuttered. I was so hungry for this man. He crashed his lips onto mine, and we fought to get our clothes off as he licked and sucked on my nipples, giving each breast equal attention.

"You're so fucking beautiful," he muttered while placing kisses from my lips to my neck. He lifted me up into his arms, and I pointed out where my bedroom was. Lying me on the bed, he began trailing kisses down my until he reached my center. He moved his tongue in a circular motion over my clit, and I damn near lost my mind.

"Ohhh fuck! Javari!" I screamed, pulling his head deeper into my pussy. I wanted all of this man, and the way he sucked on my pussy is something that should be studied or taught. He applied pressure, pulling my clit between his lips and sucking on it like he was sucking the nipple on a baby bottle. Call me dick whipped all you want, but this nigga can get it anywhere at any time. He wouldn't let up, and I started cumming so hard I was trembled. He didn't even give me time to recover before slamming inside of me, and that move had me cumming again.

"So you gon' stop fucking me, shorty!" He gritted, pulling my legs over his shoulders and tearing my ass up.

"Oh my God! I'm cumming!" I screamed as he thrust in and out of me.

"Let that shit go! Fuckkkk!" He growled as he released, and I squirted so damn hard everything went black. I could feel a coolness on my face, and I blinked a few times before I could focus on him.

"You gotta stop passing out on me, beautiful. I think we might need to visit a doctor about that. But I'm glad to have you back." He smiled, kissing my lips. I have never been fucked and sucked this way. In my head, this was my nigga. I don't care what the hell he's talking about. We go together real-real bad. For the rest of the night, he fucked me senseless and I let him.

The next morning, I woke up and made breakfast for us

while Javari took a call. I placed his plate in front of him just as he ended the call.

"So, you said you and my dad were business associates? I'm assuming you're in the same line of work as him?" I loomed over at him while biting down on a piece of my bacon.

"I'm not going to lie to you about what I do, but I'm the leader of the Taleo Cartel. Your father reigned supreme in our world, and my family had been trying to do business with him for a long ass time. It wasn't until recently did we finally connect. He asked me to handle Forelli for him, and I did. Now I know why he asked me to do that, and to be honest with you, when I heard who he wanted me to take care of, my mind went back to him being the one that kidnapped you. That made my decision easier.

During that I had one of my people ask Forelli about you. Just to see if he would tell us something. At first, I didn't know how what he was saying related to you at all, but when I found out that you were Chandler's daughter, it made it so much clearer." He sat his phone on the table and pressed play on the recording.

*"Who hired you to kidnap Jade?"* A girl asked.

I'll never forget his laugh, it's triggering just to hear it.

*"They want her dead, and nothing is going to stop them from getting what they want. His own family. They want his spot, and they'll get it. They want his daughter out the way!"*

Hearing what he said, and that triggering laugh had my body shaking uncontrollably, and the tears rushed down my face. Javari stood from his seat, lifted me out of my seat like I was a baby, and he held onto me as I cried like a baby. All of my emotions just flowed out of me. I've gone through so much and losing my father just did it for me.

"I got you, beautiful. Your Pop asked me to look over you because he trusted that I'd do right by you. He had no idea that we had ties, but that just goes to show you how when everything aligns, it's meant to happen. I'll never let anything happen to you." He placed a gentle kiss on my forehead.

"I'm sorry. I'm just so emotional, and I feel so alone with my father leaving me. I don't really have any family. I know Forelli is talking about my cousins. It has to be them. I had a feeling that they were involved in my kidnapping. He didn't come out and say, but I'm sure of it. My father knew I didn't want anything to do with his empire. Javari, I was raised in this life, but he hid most of those things from me. My cousins worked closely with him, but my father confided in me weeks before he died about some things. He said that he believed that they had been stealing money and drugs from him and had been making side deals through his ports.

My cousin Marco asked him who he had planned to leave in charge of his business? And he told him everything he owned would be coming to his only child. He said right after that, I went missing a few months later. So, he felt deep down they were moving differently. If my father died, and I was dead, then everything would go to my aunt and cousins. It's a lot, and the fact that I've been back here trying to care for my dad, and having to be around them has been stressful. Now, I have to figure out what to do with his empire. I don't want things to fall and I lose it all or have wars going on out here. I'm just stressed, and I need a break," I cried, burying my head into his chest.

"I promised him that I would help you and guide you with his company and I will. Name the place and I'll take you away for a week because I need a vacation as well. Name it and we're there." He smiled, and I looked up at him.

"The apartment," Is all I said and laid back into his chest.

"What apartment! Shorty, I know damn well you're not talking about my apartment at the warehouse."

"Yep." I smiled.

"Out of all the places in the world that your wealthy ass could go. You choose to go back to a place where your ass was kidnapped and taken too?" he asked, genuinely shocked.

"I loved my lil kidnapped life. Don't knock it until you try it." I shrugged.

"Oh, I tried it, and she's fucking fye." He winked, and I nudged him as we laughed.

"The apartment it is. Are there any important papers that we need to get from your father's home?" He asked.

"No, I have everything here in my apartment. We'll need to take that with us so that I can go through most of it. A lot of his things will be handled through his attorney though," I told him. I already know that I'm a very rich woman, but I would rather have my dad back, and he could keep the thirty-two billion net worth. Once we were dressed, Javari and I headed over to my father's compound and I spoke to the staff and Jessup, my dad's security, about what I wanted in my absence. Then I went to go look for my cousins, and I found them in my dad's office.

"What are you doing?" I asked and they both jumped.

They were clearly surprised to see me, but that surprise look turned to fury when they noticed Javari walking into the room. Javari demanded attention when he walked into any room, and I just smiled because just his presence pissed Marco off.

"Taleo, this is family business. What the fuck are you doing here? You know my Unc died so that partnership we had with you is done," Marco said to him.

"I didn't go into a partnership with you, nigga. I know what your uncle wanted because we spoke right before he died. I think your attention should be on what this beauty wants." Javari nodded in my direction, but his eyes were still on Marco.

"I'm relieving you two from any business dealings with the Chandler Empire. Whatever earnings you made is all that you will get from my father's legacy. The burning questions that you've been asking since before his death, Marco, is that you two were not in his will. He didn't leave you in charge of anything. I'm also asking that you vacate this house today. As for the company, I will oversee it with the guidance of my newly appointed COO, Javari Taleo." I smiled, looking over at Javari because I hadn't said anything to him.

I knew he had his own company, but I needed him to help me, and I trusted him. It sounded crazy because I'd only known him for such a short time, but I trusted him with my life, and if I was being real honest, I loved him.

"Bitch! What! All that we did for your hoe ass! I hope—" Before Marco could get another word out, Javari was on his ass beating the hell out of him.

I'd never in my life saw a fight up close and personal. When Ramone jumped in, I was yelling for dear life for security to come in because they really tried to jump Javari, but baby, he was giving them the business. I felt like I needed to help, so I grabbed the vase on my dad's table and hit Ramone's ass upside the head just as Jessup and Angel ran into the room. They escorted them out of the house, and it took everything in me to calm Javari down.

"Before it's over, I'm killing them. I'm just letting you know right now. I'm never going to give a nigga too many chances." He was so pissed as he paced back and forth. I grabbed his hand, pulled him in for a hug, and we stood there in the middle of my dad's office until he calmed down.

Later that night, Javari and I flew back to Philadelphia on my father's private jet. Jakari and Mace flew back on the Taleo's private jet. We headed straight to the apartment, as promised.

## NIA

### *One Month Later*

I was at Jakari's house for the weekend, and we were watching a movie just spending some quality time together. Last week he and I went on a mini vacation to Miami, and this man had me stretched out from all of the sex we'd had.

"I can't wait until I get all of my things in order so that I can leave. I want this life with you so bad," I told Jakari as he wrapped his arms around me tightly.

There was something about being wrapped up in his embrace that always seemed to comfort me. For once, I felt safe. Secure. And that said a lot.

"You know, I can't even lie a few times, I've contemplated snatching your ass up and dragging you out of that house. As bad as I want this shit too, I'm just not that nigga to force a woman to leave the next nigga. So, if this is something you really want, you gon' have to handle that, shorty. I'm not cool with you going home to the next nigga."

"I wish I didn't have to either." I sniffled, and I didn't even realize that I was crying until fresh tears hit his wifebeater.

Jakari lovingly swiped my face before leaning down to kiss my lips and I swear my heart fluttered.

"Can I ask you a question?" He asked me and I nodded. "Why do you keep going back to him? I mean, most women leave when a situation no longer serves them as beneficial. I can see you're not happy so...why stay?" We locked eyes and I sighed.

"I met Dave when I was a Freshman in college. He was my first real boyfriend. My first everything, really. At first, things were great. He was present, loving, and took care of me. Then I caught him cheating and I swore that I was done. We broke up for a few months, but then he wore me down with all his promises to do better. I wasn't strong enough to walk away, so I caved.

After graduation, things got real bad. He stopped working so I've been the one carrying all the bills. The nigga is back creeping with the same bitch from before. I sleep on the couch most nights because just the sight of him makes me sick to my stomach. I've managed to stop having sex with him ever since me and you went there, but I can tell he's starting to get antsy. I'm sticking to my guns though, because I mean it when I say that I want out.

Everything that we've acquired in the last few years has been together, and I just need to figure out a way to break apart without being flat on my ass. The house is in both of our names, but everything else is fair game. I don't put it past Dave to take everything that I got. He can be downright evil sometimes," I vented as Kari carefully sat upright in the bed. I could see the vein in his neck pulsating as he stared at me through slits.

"That nigga be putting his hands on you?"

"No." I shook my head. "But—he's been acting like he will. Basically intimidating me, and like I said, I don't put it past him."

"Mann, Nia, baby, I fuck with you heavy. And I promise I won't make you do anything you're not ready for. But you gotta know that I'm not that nigga that's gonna sit back and let my woman be harmed by no bitch ass nigga. I'm also not comfortable with you going back into a space with someone that be low key trying to bully you. So, you need to handle that shit, shorty. ASAP. Otherwise, I'ma be forced to step in and do what I do, and it won't be pretty."

Smiling weakly, I climbed on his lap, forcing his back up against the headboard. My hand fished around inside of his shorts, and I like always, he was already brick hard for me. Leaning in, I gently kissed his lips before pulling back to stare at him.

"Soon. I promise."

"I'ma hold you to that."

We spent the rest of the night rolling around in the sheets in between talking and making future plans together. Never in a million years did I expect to fall so hard and so fast for another man. The way I felt about Jakari was something the R&B singers sang songs about. He was everything to me, so I knew that I needed to handle my business and figure my shit out with Dave. Quick.

---

AFTER SPENDING MOST of the night sexing Jakari, we finally passed out in the wee hours of the morning. I promised Keisha that we could get breakfast, so after I woke up, I quickly showered and dressed to head over to the restaurant to meet her. I was on cloud nine. Jakari and I have really been taking the time to get to know each other outside of the prison. I couldn't believe that he and his brother were switching in and out, but when I saw how they were eventually being treated, I knew they were powerful.

"Girl, how is your fine ass side nigga? Ion see how you do it. Ain't no way I could sit and look at Dave cockeyed, leather sideburns ass all day when I know what I got on the side. Girlll, I would be around that muthafucka blasting *New Nigga* by Tink every two minutes. 'Cause baby that song is for y'all, shatttttttt! She said '*I been fucking on him every two nights*'. Yessss, lawd she has, Tink!" Keisha fell over in the chair and we were laughing our asses off.

"Girl, you are so crazy," I laughed, but she's not lying. Jakari and I have been at like we're in heat. My feelings for him are crazy, and every time I go home to Dave, I'm sad.

I'm sad for a few reasons. I really want to be with Jakari, but Dave and I have history. I have love for him, but I'm not in love with him anymore. It's been that way before I even met Jakari, but I just didn't know how to tell him. Dave and I have been together for so long. There was a time when I wasn't working, and he took care of me. It was only six months that I was without a job, but the reality is he did it. He didn't kick me out, but he damn sure talked shit about why we couldn't do this and that. We've had issues with him cheating on me in the past, but I forgave him for it. Now look at my ass out here doing the same damn thing. Since Javari has been a free man, he'd taken me on several weekend getaways and Jamaica and Mexico were my absolute favorites. Thank God for Keisha because my friend has been working overtime to cover for me. I've been lying to Dave about where I was going and I've never been dishonest before.

This shit was getting out of hand. Jakari is getting so tired of it all. I've been asking him to allow me time to leave Dave, and he agreed. That time he overheard Dave ask me to come suck his dick, he didn't talk to me for a few days because I didn't even call him back. I was too damn embarrassed to call him. I haven't slept with Dave in months, and that's because I'm too wrapped up in Jakari. Dave is getting just as irritated because my excuses as to why I can't have sex aren't working anymore. My plan is to tell him tonight before I leave to go and stay the weekend with Jakari.

"This food is good as shit. We have to come back," I said, stuffing some French toast in my mouth. I almost choked on it when I saw the group of people walking in to be seated. Jakari and his twin brother Javari were undeniable. There were two ladies with them and I felt myself getting pissed. It looked as if they were on a double date. One girl was hanging on Jakari. I knew the difference in the two because I was connected to that man. Besides that, his brother had a more serious demeanor, and even though he was incredibly handsome, it showed.

"Ohhh, bitch! Ion know which is which, but they both look comfortable as fuck with those hoes. We can send this bitch up if you want. I got my twenty-two in my purse and my Nina on my waist," Keisha said, and I shook my head.

He still hasn't noticed me, but I plan to introduce myself. The only reason I'm going to show my ass a little is because he's always giving me ultimatums about leaving Dave. As soon as they were seated, I stood from my seat and headed in their direction.

"Hey, Jakari. So, is this how we're doing things? One minute, you want me, and the next minute, you got the next chick on your side! Fuck you!" I yelled, pissed the fuck off. He just leaned back in his seat, staring at me, not saying shit.

"Unh-Unh! I fight bitches about my brothers, and I just got them too! Yeah, it's up!" The girl that was hanging on Kari's arm jumped up.

"Zander, sit down." He pulled the girl's arm, and she sat

down. His brother sat with a smirk on his face, and the chick sitting beside him just looked on in disbelief.

"When you come for me, come with some damn respect. I'll keep doing me until you figure out your shit. Now, take that disrespectful shit away from me!" He snapped, and I quickly turned because the tears threatened to fall.

Walking back to my table, I grabbed my purse and headed for the door. Keisha had already paid the bill and was right behind me. I was so damn emotional 'til I just broke down in my best friend's arms. I thought things with us were progressing. We both confessed that we had feelings for each other and wanted to make things between us official.

He didn't bother to come out to talk to me, so I said my goodbyes to Keisha and left. It took me about twenty minutes to get home and Dave was on the couch with a frown on his face. I ignored his ass and went to lay down for a little while. My feelings were hurt as I replayed the scene in my head from earlier. Wait. Did the girl say *her brothers and that she just got them?!*

K, I feel like an idiot. That was his baby sister. He told me all about them just finding out they had a sister. I feel like a damn fool. I immediately pulled my phone out and dialed his number, but he didn't answer, so I sent him a text.

> Me: I'm so sorry for jumping to conclusions.

> Babe: If you want to do immature shit like that, you might as well stay with that fuck nigga you're fighting so hard to stay with. Don't call my phone again unless you ready for me. I'm not playing this back and forth shit with you. And this sneaking shit for me is over., I'm Jakari Taleo, the fuck I look like sneaking to be with a woman I love.

> Me: Jakari, I'm sorry. I love you too, baby.

He never responded, and I was going crazy. What the fuck have I done?

# JAKARI

IT'S BEEN a few days since the incident with Nia at the restaurant. She pissed me off with that shit. Zander and Jade fucked with me all day about Nia after we left breakfast. She's been calling and texting, and even though she pissed me off, I missed her lil' jealous ass. But I meant what I said. If she's not ready to come to me, we're not doing this shit anymore.

"You good, bro?" Javari asked as we sat in one of our other warehouses watching Jade's cousins, Marco and Ramone, and Trevor Sandoval.

"Yeah, I'm cool." I'm glad we're about to deal with these niggas because I'm tired of hearing their fucking names. Since we'd partnered with the Chandler Cartel, everything for us has evolved, and the Taleo Cartel is untouchable. Javari has had people on Jade's folks for a minute now, and their moves got sloppy because shit was getting uneasy for them. Jade had stopped them from working. So when we heard they were in

185

Philadelphia to meet with our rivals to take us out, we wanted to make shit easy for them and welcome them the city of Brotherly love.

"You know I can't stand a pussy nigga. You know I'm not going to even make this a long ass process because what you niggas did to your own blood is some wicked bullshit and you need to burn in hell for what you did. You muthafuckas are the epitome of what greed looks like. Drop these pussy niggas and send their fucking ashes to the bitch that birthed these pussies. She's lucky her niece wants her to live. Otherwise, she would be right here with you since she agreed with y'all hurting Jade.

Yeah, we know everything, It's crazy what kind of information a fat ass, and beautiful face can get you," Javari said to them, as Sammy walked into the room and Ramone's eyes widened.

Sammy is one of our women that we send out to get next to these niggas when we need information that we might not get through other channels. Sometimes a fat ass, will get that information quicker. Since Sammy is on our staff, she was the perfect person, and it didn't take long for her to get what we needed. She had Ramone eating out the palm of her hands, with his thirsty ass. She was able to get bugs planted in their apartment and their mom's home. Now these niggas were hanging from these chains as our people were lowering them down closer to the raging fire in the inferno.

"Fuckkk! Nooooo please!" Ramone screamed as the heat hit his ass.

"Mone, shut the fuck up and take the shit, nigga. Don't let these pussies see you sweat. Fuck Jade! I hope that bitch burn in hell, fucking cunt!" Marco yelled.

"You first, my nigga!" Javari dropped the chain. That nigga fell headfirst into the fire and he screamed until his screams went silent.

"Sandoval, you should have just stayed your ass on your side and just been the fuck mad because we killed your bitch by ass brother. Now I'ma send you to meet his bitch ass, and if any of you other family members wanna run up, well, they will be met with the same fate."

"Drop them!" Jav yelled, and when the chain was released one by one, they fell into the fire. I'm just glad this shit was over. Jade needed to rest and feel comfortable about moving around. She went out, but for the most part, she stayed in that damn apartment, and it's become a clutch for her.

I walked outside because I really needed some air. This shit with Nia was fucking with me because I really loved the girl. This shit came fast and unexpected. Mace and Jakari came walking out of the warehouse.

"Nigga, I think you need to find new ways to kill people forreal. That last nigga smelt like he ate too much damn pork. This shit be stank and bad on my stomach." His nose was turned up and I burst out laughing.

"You really get on my nerves." Jav shook his head.

"What's up?" Jav asked me.

"I'm just tired of this back and forth with Nia. I'm ready to let that go because she's still over there with her nigga, and I'm just not built for that." I shrugged.

"Nigga, I can't believe you been a side nigga for this long. I never thought I'd see it. All that money and power, and your ass is out here hiding on the side of the house waiting for her to take the trash out so you can get a kiss goodnight. Nah, nigga. Nah, ain't that much good pussy in the world. If I was you, I'd go show that nigga who the fuck you are. Bust up in that bitch and get yo' woman. Y'all call me and let me know how that shit go though 'cause I'ma about to go home." Mace patted me on the back and walked to his truck.

"All that and you're not going with us?" Javari asked him.

"No, nigga. I'm not going to them people house to steal that man girl," Mace yelled out. Even though I knew he was joking around about going to get Nia, I was ready to do just that.

"Sometimes we gotta step off the throne just to handle shit ourselves," Javari said to me, and I nodded.

An hour later, we were back in the city and pulling up to Nia's house. Either shit gonna go smooth or it'll go left. Whichever way it goes, it's up. Our guards stayed behind, but Javari and I jumped out of the car. I had already sent Nia a text, but she never answered. The closer we got to the door, I could hear arguing.

"I thought you were supposed to be in Miami with Keisha! Bitch, you was with this nigga!" He screamed.

"I know you didn't put your hands on me!" Nia screamed.

*Whap!*

I kicked the fucking door in and rushed that nigga, unleashing all my fucking rage on his ass. He tried to fight back, but I caught him off guard, and he didn't have a chance.

"Jakari! What...Wait, what are you doing?" Nia's voice snapped me out of it, and Javari pulled me off this nigga. When I turned and saw the bruise on her face, I stomped that pussy out. Maybe I'm wrong for running up in their shit, but fuck this nigga!

"Nia, go pack a bag. Get whatever you need because you're not coming back to this nigga." She stared at me for a minute and then turned to go pack her shit. Now, if she'd said she wanted to stay with him, I would've left her here with him.

I leaned my face closer to the bitch nigga sprawled out on the floor coughing up blood. I could see the fear all in his eyes which enraged me even more because he was real tough with a woman.

"Stay the fuck away from her. Don't call, don't text. Pretend she don't even exist. This is your one and only warning, nigga or yo' mama gonna be wearing that face on a t-shirt. Fuck with me if you want to." For good measure, I delivered another kick to the nigga's face, and he passed out.

When Nia came back downstairs with a few bags, I

thought she'd trip out when she saw the nigga unconscious, but instead, she stepped right over him and waltzed out the front door. She better had.

# JADE

***Four Months Later***

I NEEDED this time away from it all, and I'm so happy I didn't rush back to Las Vegas. I'm not sure when I'll go back to deal with my affairs there. All I know is I thank God for Javari Taleo. I can't believe that my cousins and aunt went through so many lengths to destroy their closest family. My dad did everything for them and loved his sister and her kids more than life. He would've never left them out here starving, which is why he raised Marco and Ramone up in his business.

It may not have been the ideal business for most families, but this was our family. He made them rich, and they never had to work another day in their lives if they didn't want to. That just goes to show you that when greed takes over your soul, you become evil and deceitful. I loved Marco and Ramone. Before all of this, they were my favorite people. Had I not found out about their wrongdoings before my dad passed, I would've allowed them to step into the role of leader of the Chandler Cartel.

Then to find out that they were meeting with the Sandoval Cartel to kill Javari, Jakari, and me just solidified my decision in cutting them off. I guess they were upset about what happened when I told them that their services were no longer needed. Javari was smart to put some of his people on them. We found out so much more. To find out that my aunt knew what they were doing and she had no objections that shit was crazy to me.

"Morning, beautiful." Javari walked into the kitchen, wrapping his arms around me and placing kisses on my neck. He splits his time here at the warehouse with me and time at his home because he has his daughter. Ciani is just the cutest little thing, and we've bonded so well. That's my little diva girl; she's always calling me pretty, and I'm always saying the same about her. I've found myself shopping for her when I'm shopping for myself.

I never thought a child would bring so much joy to my life, but she has. We go out to eat often, but Chick-fil-A is our favorite, and we both love Coldstone ice cream. We wear Javari our with that because he's always picking it up for us or having someone go get it. I'm really hands-on with taking care of myself. I don't like all of the chefs and maids but I under-stand why he needs it. I've stayed at his home a few nights and that place is absolutely beautiful. I haven't made any decisions about my life, but I knew that I wanted to live here and be with him. Javari and I just kind of fell into this space together and took our time just to learn each other. It's been an amazing time, and I don't want to be anywhere else but right here with him.

"Morning, are you hungry?" I asked him.

"I'll take some coffee. We can just do lunch since we're going to the mall with Nia and Javari. Remember, we're having seafood night at my mom's later," he said, kissing me again before taking his coffee and having a seat.

"Is Ciani having a great time at Uncle Jakari's house?" I asked him. Ci has been over there for the last few days because her aunt Zander is there. Zander is such a beautiful person and oh my God, she loves her brothers. It's taking Javari a little more time with her than Jakari, but he's coming around. She and I have become really close; she calls me every day, and I just love her spirit. She brings life to any room. She's wealthy and has so many goals. I'm rooting for her for sure. Can't wait to see her walk across that stage as a doctor. The intercom buzzed, and Javari answered it.

"Yeah?"

"Good morning, sir. We're here to crop the weed plants, but I need for you to come out here for a minute," the guy said, and he walked out back. I grabbed my basket because hearing that they were going to be taking the weed damn near broke my heart. I threw on some shorts and a shirt and ran out back. Javari was standing there shaking his head, and I stopped in my tracks, giggling. They were looking at my garden. It had started to grow. I even had some little green tomatoes coming up. I still had a long way to go, but I was excited. Oh, and I never moved my shit, I left it right there in the weed pasture. I just acted as if I moved it.

"Jade baby, what do you expect for me to do with this garden? You have the shit in my pasture," Javari fussed and shrugged with my lips pouted.

"Cut around it, and don't cut all the weed. I still need my supply. As a matter of fact, can you help me put some in my basket?" I looked over at him. He just stood there shaking his head, but he grabbed my basket and had the worker fill it for me.

"Just do your best to cut around it and leave some with the garden," he advised, and I jumped up and down.

"Let's go get dressed." He smacked me on my ass and we headed back inside.

A couple of hours later, we were out the door and heading over to Javari's house. When we got there, he and Nia were in the family room waiting on Zander and Ciani. I love Nia and Kari together. They look so good together and she's settling in well with him. Our first introduction wasn't the best, but if she was operating off the same thing I was with Javari, sis, I understand.

I still say his wife was an idiot, but maybe sis just wanted something different. I thank her though, because if he was still married, things would've never gone this way with us. Maybe business partners, but definitely not us being together.

When Zander and Ciani came walking downstairs, we all fell out laughing because Zander had her dressed just like her in a cute jean skirt, a beige stretch top, with a jean vest on and some Gucci tights. Oh my goodness, they looked so cute. But what had us in a fit of laughter is Zander had light makeup on Ciani, and her little lips were glossed to the gloss gawds.

"Yesssss, Ciani!" Nia and I blurted full of laughter. She strutted her little self around the room to model with her aunt, and we were no good. The only one that wasn't laughing was her daddy.

"Ci, you look like you can fry chicken on your lips. Take some off, baby girl," he spoke softly to her. I loved the way he handled her.

"But I like it, daddy and Aunt Zanny said I'm so pretty with it on. I love Aunt Zanny, daddy. She bought me all these clothes, and we're going to get some more Gucci slides at the mall." She clapped.

"Zander, she's almost seven. Tone it down just a little bit," he told his sister.

"Ok, I'm sorry." Zander apologized, and I saw the flash of sadness in her eyes. I hoped that her brother really sat down with her. I think he saw that same sadness because he just stared at her as she and Ciani walked off.

"Nigga, you need to get it together. She loves us and wants to be close to you." Jakari was right. It was written all over her that she wanted to be close to her brother.

Once everyone was ready to go, it didn't take us long to

get to the mall. For hours, we went from store to store, and the girls were having a blast, but the guys... uhhh, not so much.

"Daddyyyyy! Five Guys! I want a hamburger," Ci jumped up and down. I have never had a burger from there, but I wanted to try since her and Zander were so hype about it.

"Sup, Zander?" some guy spoke to her.

"Don't speak to me. I don't speak to dudes that call me out of my name, Bricks." Zander spat, and Javari's head turned in their direction and reacted quickly.

"The next time you open your fucking mouth to call my sister a bitch will be the last time you speak, bitch!" he exclaimed.

"Yesssss, brother! Tell his ass, and I got two of 'em, nigga." Zander pointed in Jakari's direction as he and Nia walked up on us.

"Who is this?" he asked, looking from his brother to Brick's.

"The nigga that called Zander a bitch," Javari spoke.

"If you see her, go the other direction. Because I promise our next conversation won't be as nice. The death toll will go up by one when I kill your ass," Jakari gritted in his face. The boy had a mug on his face, but he didn't respond. I'm glad Nia had already pulled Zander and Ciani away. The guys gathered their composure. We walked over to Five Guys, and Ciani was jumping up and down.

"Mommy. Mommy! Daddy, look! It's Mommy!" she

pointed at the girl that was pulling fries from the hot oil. Javari stared at the woman, and I knew it was his ex-wife. She tried her best to ignore her daughter, but Ciani started to cry. Whatever they were going through, this baby didn't ask for it.

"Javari, allow her to at least speak to her. Ciani doesn't understand all of this," I whispered. He grabbed Ciani's hand and pulled her closer to the counter.

"Tori, it's ok to speak to your daughter," he told her, and when she turned, it was evident that she missed her child.

"Hey, Ci Ci. I miss you so much, baby," she said, wiping the tears from her eyes.

"Tori, what the fuck you crying for? That's our fucking daughter, and nigga, I'm coming for mine. You think you got the upper hand but bitch, it's up, and that's on everything I love and my daughter!" This dude jumped in Javari's face and all hell broke loose.

"Tarell, let it go. Please don't do this in front of my daughter." Tori begged the guy. She quickly ran from behind the counter, trying to pull him away. But before she could, Javari was in his face. We pleaded with him not to show out in this mall with his daughter here, and thank God he listened. Thank God for Jakari being here to control it.

"I'll see you soon," Is all he said to the guy, and we all walked off. Zander and Ciani were escorted out by the guards. After things calmed down, we went back to his mother's house, and we enjoyed a day with the family.

"I never thought I would see the day that both of my sons would be here with their significant others and happy."

"Ma, Jade and I are just taking things slow right now," Javari told her.

"Boy, hush. That's your woman and she makes you happy. This is the happiest I've seen you in years. Live your life; don't let it pass you by, son. It's ok to open up to love again. Especially when God sends her to you. You all met under some crazy circumstances, but it was meant to happen," she said to him, and he turned to look over at me. I appreciated how Ms. Chance loved her sons and loved on Nia, and I as well. We sat around, ate and had a time. We were about to play a game, and Javari's cousins walked into the room. Zander damn near lost her mind over Gazi Black.

"Lawd, is he my cousin or just your cousin because he's beautiful?" She gazed at him, and Nia and I had to agree.

"Cut that beautiful shit out, lil mama. But you fine as fuck, and hell no, we're not related. The only way that you'll be related to me is when I marry your ass." He kissed Zander's cheek and her ass was standing there stuck. Nia and I laughed so damn hard because he about to do her in.

Chance and Stacia definitely did their big one with their sons. They're so handsome, but my favorite is Javari Taleo. I sat at the table eating, but the moment I placed a piece of fish in my mouth, I took off for the bathroom. I was sick as hell and all my food came up.

"Jade, are you alright, baby?" Javari ran into the bathroom.

"She'll be fine. She's just pregnant, that's all," Ms. Chance said, walking into the bathroom with us to get a cold rag for my face. Me and Javari were just staring at her because pregnant? Oh hell no. But come to think about it, we haven't used any damn protection.

"I just sent the guard to the store; he'll be back in a minute."

Once I got myself together, we went back out to join the family. "Girl, do you think you're pregnant?" Nia asked, pulling me to the side.

"I mean, it's possible. But I guess I'll need to go to the doctor. This is insane because I'm sitting here thinking of the possibilities." I smiled.

"I'm so happy for you if you are. Maybe we can have a double baby shower," Nia said to me and my neck snapped up so damn quick.

"Noooooo way!" I shouted.

"Yes, we were waiting to tell everyone, but when you rushed out of here throwing up, and Ms. Chance said she thought you were pregnant, we decided to let the cat out of the bag." Nia smiled.

"How do you feel about it?" I questioned, genuinely happy for her.

"I've never been this happy in my life. I love that man, and I'm so glad he came and got me out of that house. Girl, I left everything behind and gave no fucks about it. Jakari Taleo is everything I need, and finding out that we're having a baby just brought us closer together." She smiled and I gave her a hug.

"Congratulations." I smiled as we joined the rest of the family.

"Nia and I are having a baby," Jakari blurted out, and we burst into laughter as everyone jumped up in excitement.

"Ohhh my goodness! I'm having two grandbabies! This is the best news ever," Ms. Chance gushed.

Javari and I decided to take the pregnancy test that the guard went out and got me at home. Now, we both were sitting here staring at the results. I'm pregnant.

"How do you feel?" I asked him, a little nervous because he was so quiet.

"I can't even tell you how happy I am right now. We didn't plan it, but we damn sure didn't prevent it. I love you, beautiful." He leaned in to kiss my lips, and one thing led to another. And for the rest of the night, we celebrated our way. I loved this man, and he truly saved my life.

## JAKARI

### *Five Months Later*

Nia and I were excited about the arrival of our daughter and couldn't wait to meet her. One thing that we both agreed on is not having our daughter without being married. I wanted it, and so did she, so we had a small ceremony and got married a few days ago. I can't believe that we're here in this moment, but I'm happy about it. Sometimes things don't go the way you plan them, but I'm happy as fuck that I took my ass to prison. That story on how I met my wife will forever go down in history.

My wife is beautiful. She makes me happy, her heart was pure, and the way she loves me speaks volumes. The business is doing well, and things have calmed down to the point that we've been able to relax a little.

Javari and I were at the INC meeting last night, and everyone congratulated us on the merger between the Taleo Cartel and the Chandler Cartel. It was a big move, but Javari decided to allow members of the INC to move through our ports if they wanted to, which would enlarge their Cartels as well—a win for everyone involved.

"Babe, I think something is wrong." Nia walked into the family room holding her stomach.

"Are you in labor, babe?" I jumped up.

"I'm not sure, but it's not time yet!" She cried. I didn't want to take any chances, so I grabbed our things and we headed out.

"Jakari, please help me, babe! It hurts!" Nia screamed, and Chris, my guard, moved through the city streets as fast as he could. By the time we got inside the hospital lobby, Nia's water broke, and she was contracting back-to-back. We both were worried about the baby coming early.

"I'm here with you, baby." I kissed her lips as they rushed her up to labor and delivery. I sent my family a group text because I didn't have time to call everyone.

Nia cried as she dug her nails into my arm as contractions hit her back-to-back.

"Kari, I'm so scared. What if something is wrong?" Her voice trembled as she cried into my arms.

"Listen to me, beautiful. You got this. Our daughter is strong and so are you. We got this." Nurses and doctors rushed into the room to check to see how far she dilated.

"It's time. She's already ten centimeters," the nurse stated, and minutes later, Nia's doctor walked into the room.

"Nia, stop worrying. We're a little early but it's ok for her to come," she said, and we both relaxed a little bit.

"I can't do this! It's killing me!" she cried.

"Can she get something for pain?" I questioned as Nia held onto my hand for dear life.

"No, she's dilated too far. It's time to push, Nia. On the next contraction, push," the doctor told her, and on the next contraction, she pushed.

"Give me one more push, Nia! Come on, Nia! Pushhh-hh!" the doctor coached her.

"Urgghhhh!" She pushed and my daughter was out. They let me cut the cord, and I was so damn emotional. This woman just gave birth to my whole heart in human form.

Aleah Chance Taleo was 6lb, 12 ounces, and 20 inches long, and our daughter was a beautiful mix of both of us.

"She's so beautiful." Nia cried, admiring her.

"Just like her mother." We sat for a while bonding with our daughter, and once they got them both cleaned up, the family came in to see us. Everyone was so excited to meet our new addition, and my mom just couldn't get enough of her granddaughter. Nia's parents just left to go back home but called and said they would be here this coming weekend. Life was good. My wife and daughter was healthy and happy, and just as long as they're good, I'm good. I thank God for my blessings.

## EPILOGUE

### JAVARI

I DIDN'T EXPECT my life to end up like this. I never imagined myself not being married to Tori or her telling me that Ciani isn't my daughter. There were clearly red flags, but instead of taking heed to them, I ignored them. I'm not going to lie; Tori was it for me, and I would've never disrespected or mistreated her. I loved the ground that woman walked on, so when all of this hit me, it fuckin' hit me.

I haven't spoken or seen Tori since the Five Guys incident, and I really didn't talk to her then. I haven't asked why she did what she did, and to be honest, I don't want to know why. Hearing her bullshit ass excuse would only piss me off. I can't tell you how many nights I got up and walked out of the house with my gun in hand, ready to find this girl and blow her fucking brains out. There is nothing that she could do or say that would make me understand her logic. She's just a disloyal bitch. If you're not happy in your marriage or relationship, just leave.

Why would you stay in something that's not fulfilling to you? Now this is the nigga that's supposed to be Ciani's Pop? Nah, fuck them! I told that nigga he would see me soon and that's exactly what the fuck I meant. I owe that nigga a bullet, and I'm here to pay my muthafuckin' debt. I'm never going to be ok with that nigga breathing the same air as me in my city. I decided to do this one on my own. No one knew I was here. I could hear their voices, keys jingling, and the lock turning.

"I guess I can get some rest tonight since your cousin got Braylyn," Tori said to him. I forgot all about her deceitful ass being pregnant and having her baby.

"I gotta make a run; I'm just dropping you off. I got some moves to make, because we need some money coming in. Your pussy ass ex really fucked my money up, and that's why we planning to get that nigga. You just be ready to get our daughter when it's time. I got this nigga out of D.C. that's going to front me some weight," his punk ass said to her.

"Tarell, I think it's best that you leave him alone. I don't want to be involved in that. I lost my daughter because I wasn't being honest. I would like to see her again, and if you keep bothering him, he won't let me see her again. I love you, but you're not on his level. He's not in the streets, Tarell. He's a damn Cartel Boss. He has shooters, guards, and assassins; he has drug plants, for God sakes. Your definition of being the plug and his is different."

*Whap!*

"Bitch, shut the fuck up! Taking up for that nigga in my shit." He gripped her neck, and I'd heard enough.

"I'm glad you two decided to join me." As soon as they heard my voice, he tried to run, but I sent a shot to his leg that halted his stride, and he hit the floor.

"Ja...Javari, please. Please don't hurt me. I've just been trying to stay out the way. I haven't done anything or plotted anything with him. I tried calling you several times to warn you, but you never answered my calls. I'm sorry, please don't hurt me. I want to see Ciani, and I have another daughter now," she begged. I ignored her for now because I needed her nigga to hear me.

"You thought that I would allow you to keep breathing. You thought that I wouldn't know what you were planning? Bitch, you're a lil' fish playing with a fuckin' shark! You'll never win! And that's my daughter, bitch!" I gripped both of my guns and emptied my clips in his ass.

That was me letting all of my aggression out on his ass. This nigga played a part in destroying my family. The only reason Tori is still alive is because of our daughter. Ciani loves her mother, and I don't want to hurt my child in that way. She stood shaking and crying and I felt nothing for her.

"The only reason you're alive is because of Ciani. I don't even care that you witnessed this because you know what I'll do to you even if I'm locked up. It's best that you start over from here, and when I'm in a better space, I'll think about a relationship with your daughter. It'll always be supervised. I'll never feel comfortable enough for you to have her. Maybe that'll change, but for now, nah, that's not happening. Someone will be here to clean this up." I dropped a duffle bag on her table and walked out. It was the money that she kept in a duffle bag, just in case of emergencies. That night I closed one chapter and welcomed my new one.

---

### One Year Later

I TOGGLED BACK and forth with the idea of getting a DNA test done, but what for? Ci is still my child and that's the end of that. I decided to sell my home, and Jade and I built a new one for our family. Since Jade loved my apartment so much, I decided to recreate everything she loved about it right on our compound. I also bought into the cold stone franchise and had one built as well. Our compound was her escape, and I loved that for her.

Jade gave birth to our twins, our son Aiden, and daughter Jaidyn and I swear my heart is so full. I guess one of us had to have a set of twins. Since Jakari had a daughter, yeah, I guess it had to be me. I didn't think I could get into another relationship, and it was damn sure hard to say the words. Not going to lie; it wasn't until she got pregnant that I realized I would do anything for her. I needed time to get my mind right. I needed time to get my heart right and she gave me that while still loving me. I'm grateful for the blessings. Our life is so complete, and I can't wait to see her raise our babies. Ciani loves being a big sister, and I love that.

I never thought this day would come. Our entire family was here on a small island in the Maldives. Today is the day I marry the love of my life.

"Look at my baby! Son, you've overcome so much, and I'm so proud of you. I'm so glad that you allowed love in. Jade is your one, and I love her as if I gave birth to her. She has no hidden agendas. She loves you for you." She smiled, kissing me on my cheek.

"Thank you, mom. I love you."

A few minutes later, it was time for me to go down, and I've never been more ready. Just as I opened the door, there stood my beautiful bride.

"Hey, baby! Oh, my goodness, you look good enough to

eat. But I'm not here for that right now. This is my attorney and friend, Kelcie Pierce. Kelcie has some documents for us to sign, and I just need for you to pay me a dollar." She held out her hand, and I wasn't sure if I had a dollar. Walking over to my money clip, I pulled a hundred-dollar bill from it and handed it to her.

"This is all I have," I told her.

"I'll take it." She put the money inside of her bra and had the biggest smile on her face. This woman was amazingly beautiful, but I was standing here confused as hell.

"Javari, thank you for being my peace. Thank you for saving me. Thank you for loving me without limits. Thank you for taking care of my heart. This is what love is supposed to look like. I'll love and honor you forever! This document makes you the owner and leader of the Chandler Cartel. I'll receive a ten percent payment of its yearly net income, and each one of my children will receive ten percent of the yearly income to their trust funds. So that's forty percent our way and sixty daddy's way."

I couldn't believe this woman. She loved my baby girl like she was hers, and that just made me love her even more.

"Thank you, baby. I don't know what to say but know that I'll make your father proud. Now let's go get married." I smiled, stealing a kiss.

Twenty minutes later, the wedding had started, and the beach was beautifully set. There was a glass stage built for us to walk down the aisle. Each side of the stage had guests from our family, friends, and members of the INC and their guests. The stage was filled with white roses and candles. They executed the look perfectly.

The wedding party entered, and when Zander walked in, I smiled. She was beautiful. I waited until she got up front and stepped up to stop her.

"You look beautiful, baby sister. I love you." Kissing her cheek, she wrapped her arms around my neck as a single tear fell from her eyes. This past year, we've spent a lot of time together, and I've grown to really love her. The wedding party was small. Jade only had Nia and Zander, and I had my brother and Mace. Ciani was our flower girl, and she looked absolutely adorable.

Right after the mall situation, I had a sit down with my baby sister and explained how my coldness had nothing to do with her and everything to do with our Pop. Thankfully, she understood and didn't bear a grudge. We even had a conversation about her mother's part in our father's infidelity. I kept it real and told Zander that I wasn't comfortable with her being around. I understood that was still her mother, but she wasn't no kin to me. I would never disrespect or put my own mom in an environment that she wasn't comfortable in. So for now, she just had to sit it out.

Surprisingly, Zander understood, and so far, we haven't had any issues. I truly loved my little sister, and despite my Pop's disloyalty, she was a big blessing to the family. Even my mom loved her, which said a lot.

*First Time* by Teeks started playing, and she took my breath away. When she made it down the aisle, we were both in tears. This moment is something we'll never forget. When we gathered ourselves, the pastor started the ceremony, and an hour later, we were married.

"Oh, babe, this island is beautiful. I'm so in love with it," she said and I had to agree with her.

"You're right, and since we're giving out gifts... this house and the island belongs to you. I love you, Mrs. Taleo," I said to her, placing soft, sensual kisses on her lips as we danced to *Whenever Wherever Whatever* by Maxwell.

"Oh, my Goddd! Really, babbbby?! Will I be able to grow my weed here?" she asked, and I laughed so fucking hard. I married a pothead.

"If we can't, I'll have it flown in from our private tomato and cabbage garden."

"Yesssss, that's some boss shit. Thank you, Mr. Taleo." She excitedly wrapped her arms around my neck, kissing my lips. I was ready to get out of here and put another baby in my wife. I truly couldn't believe she signed over her father's empire to me. This is bigger than anything that I could've imagined.

When I told her I'd make her father proud, I meant that. The allegiance that I'm building will be talked about for decades and decades. A power move that will shake the world. So many deals will be made, and territories will expand. No matter how high the Taleo's climb, one thing is true. I'll always stand on the shoulders of the INC. That's what my Pop built and made us who we are today.

For the rest of the evening, we enjoyed our time with our family and friends. I thank God for bringing this woman to me. She's indeed my peace.

## The End

## CONNECT WITH AUTHOR K. RENEE

**To get VIP access of new releases, and sneak peeks please join my mailing list.**

Text KRENEE to 22828

**Facebook:** https://www.facebook.com/karen.renee.9421450

**Instagram:** http://www.instagram.com/Authorkrenee

Made in the USA
Monee, IL
01 March 2025

13174307R00125